BEST GIRL

BEST GIRL

Doris Buchanan Smith

Viking

VIKING
Published by the Penguin Group
Penguin Books USA Inc., 375 Hudson Street, New York, New York 10014, U.S.A.
Penguin Books Ltd, 27 Wrights Lane, London W8 5TZ, England
Penguin Books Australia Ltd, Ringwood, Victoria, Australia
Penguin Books Canada Ltd, 10 Alcorn Avenue,
Toronto, Ontario, Canada M4V 3B2
Penguin Books (N.Z.) Ltd, 182–190 Wairau Road, Auckland 10, New Zealand

Penguin Books Ltd, Registered Offices: Harmondsworth, Middlesex, England

First published in 1993 by Viking, a division of Penguin Books USA Inc.

10 9 8 7 6 5 4 3 2 1

Library of Congress Cataloging-in-Publication Data
Smith, Doris Buchanan.
Best girl / by Doris Buchanan Smith   p.   cm.
Summary: As she struggles to cope with a difficult mother and
finding her place in the world, young Nealy Compton finds solace in
the relative solitude and safety beneath her neighbor's porch.
I S B N   0 - 6 7 0 - 8 3 7 5 2 - 0
[1. Mothers and daughters—Fiction.] 2. Family problems—Fiction
3. Self-acceptance—Fiction.] I. Title.
PZ7.S64474Be 1993 [Fic]—dc20   92-25931 CIP AC

Printed in U.S.A
Set in 11 point ITC Garamond Book

This is for Joan Millman,
who came from Boston to be with me.

This is the naming of the names
of those who brought
tea and sympathy,
solace and sandwiches,
muscle and blood and survival sass,
during the resurrection of my house in 1984–1985.

First, the neighbors who called the fire department,
Linda Royster and the Lambrights,

Next, the fire fighters
and the police investigators,

Then those who shoveled soot,
Jonee Ansa, Tina McElroy Ansa, Frankie Bulfer, Jingle
Davis, John Habich, and my daughter, Susan Smith.

Those involved with the rebuilding were
Larry Bryson who helped me with the plans,
Jim Pearson and Cy Flenchum who did the major work
and were my "family" in those days,
Kurt Spaethe who took up where they left off,
James Crosby who installed the heating and
air conditioning units,
Roy Rosenbalm who plumbed,
all of whom became supportive,
rebuilding buddies for the duration.
Also, Tommy and the Two-Tones,
who painted the exterior,
and the rocking Sheetrockers,
who did an admired-by-all job with walls and ceilings.

And myriad others:

Mother, Dad in one of his last independent journeys,
Claudia Thompson, the Queens, Beth Engel,
Mike and Deedee Henley, and Katie, who
watched from her stroller,
sons Matt Smith and Willie Cunningham,
Pat Bartlett, Seabert and Ione Parsons,
Nancy Simpson, Lorraine Ruhl, Neil Conrad,
Daisy and George Large, Betty McCann,
Carolyn Johnson, Janice Moore, Bettie Sellers,
Alex Zimmermacher, Stace McDaniel, Carolyn McMillan,
Patty and Ken Muse, Helen Lenkerd and
friends from Druid Hills
Baptist Church in Atlanta.

If, from the lapsing memory of time
I have left anyone out, please feel thanked
and know you are included.

THIS BOOK IS FOR EACH OF YOU!

Contents

BEST GIRL

1

Fire!

Nealy Compton was not under Mrs. Dees's house the night it burned.

From her bedroom there was a series of *poof* sounds, more felt than heard. She bounded into the living room saying, "What's that?" Stretched out on the sofa, thumbing through *TV Guide,* Mama didn't acknowledge the *poofs* or Nealy.

Another *poof* shook the house, and Nealy reached for the doorknob.

"Don't you dare open that door," Mama said. When Nealy hesitated, Mama added, "If you go out that door, don't ever come back through it." Two days earlier, Mama had said the same words to Noel Anne during an argument. Noel Anne had gone and not come back and Nealy had been part of the reason for the fuss.

There was another *poof,* and Nealy reached for the curtain. When she pulled it back, fire was at her nose.

"Mama! Fire!"

Mama sprang to the window, jumped away, leaped to the phone.

From the windows of Mrs. Dees's house across the street, a fire raged. Fierce orange flames.

Before Mama finished dialing, they heard sirens.

Another *poof,* and fire leaped out the windows. Above the ravenous roar of fire, Nealy heard the tinkle of glass in the street.

"Oh, my word!" Mama said, back at the window. "Do you see her—Mrs. Dees?"

"She's gone," Nealy said, eyes wide, shaking her head in awe of the hungry fire. "She's out of town." Thank goodness she'd seen her go, had seen her take the cat, too. The fire was terrifying. Thank goodness she didn't have to be terrified for Mrs. Dees's life, or the cat's.

She pressed her mouth against the cool glass. The fire was framed by the windows, broiling inside and reaching out, as though to reach across for her. The yards here, their front yard and Mrs. Dees's side yard, were very small. Not much more than the street separated the two houses.

Three fire trucks screamed around the corner, and Nealy was out the door.

Mama's "Don't you dare!" pierced her back as the heat of the fire stung her face and nose. She knew how serious Mama's "don't you dare" could be, but she had to go. It was her house, too.

Fire fighters tugged at both ends of the hose, taking one end toward the fire hydrant, the nozzle end toward the house. Two of the fire fighters grabbed a ladder, flung it against the edge of the porch roof, and scrambled up. They disappeared into the dark above the fire and reappeared almost instantly as the roof lit up from the fire below.

"No one is home!" Nealy yelled. "No one is in the house." That would be the most important thing for them to know, that no one was there. She pushed her way through the already-gathered crowd, trying to let the fire fighters know. Hoses were spewing water with no seeming effect. The crowd took up the "no one home" call until there was a police officer grabbing Nealy's elbow.

"How do you know no one is here?" he asked,

leaning down to hear above the fire and the engines and the crowd.

"She went out of town. I saw her leave. She took her cat."

"Are you sure?"

"Yes."

"That's right," someone added. "Her car is gone. If she was here, her car would be here." It was Mr. Lyle. This situation was so unreal, Nealy was startled to see the faces of people she knew. The Lyles, the Kennedys, Ms. Royster, everyone from the neighborhood and strangers from beyond.

"Aren't you Dave Compton's girl?" the officer asked.

"Yes," she said. "Is Daddy here?"

"Nah. Not his shift tonight."

Quite suddenly the light from the fire dimmed, the house no longer aflame but just aglow. Spotlights brightened the night, lighting the house from the outside. Fire fighters passed behind the windows, pitching smoldering furniture onto the porch. The windows were no longer orange from the fire inside, but white, from searchlights shining in.

Nealy's throat was so lumpy and dry that even

her swallow was dry, and so were her eyes. Parched, as though she herself had been too close to the fire.

The tossed-out furniture on the porch glowed. Light flared occasionally within the house from the fire fighters' flashlights or the fire suddenly licking out, trying to start again. A stream of water quickly doused these flames, both in the house and on the porch. The crowd sighed a collective sigh, buzzed, and mumbled. Nealy still stood, staring. So it was burned, this house. Her house.

A hubbub arose in the crowd. "A body." "Footprints." "They found a body in the house." Nealy clamored to find out more. Who could it be? Mrs. Dees's children were grown and lived out of town. Could one of them have been here?

Finally, one fire truck chugged away, then another, leaving one fire truck and several fire fighters to attend to ghost flames that spurted here and there, just from the heat. When the two fire engines disappeared, the crowd began drifting away. The remaining fire fighters tromped back and forth, in and out, then sat on the porch talking.

"If they get the wet debris out, I think they can save most of the floor," one of them said.

What a weird thing to say. Nealy didn't see that anything could be saved. What was the point?

She edged up to the steps to ask the question she was anxious to ask. "Did you find someone inside? A body?"

"No, no, no," a fire fighter said quickly. "There was no one inside. The woman is out of town."

Yes, she knew that. She was the one who'd told them. Instead of being reassured, she wondered if they didn't want to tell her. She was just a kid, after all.

"How do you know?" Wasn't it possible that, in all the rush and rubble, they might not have found someone? She shuddered, thinking of what a crisp such a person would be by now.

"Oh, we know," a slickered, booted, hatted fire fighter said. "You smell it."

Not understanding, wanting to know, Nealy asked, "Smell what?"

"Flesh burning."

Her nose wrinkled, and she was sorry she had asked. In a few more minutes, she herself drifted away, one of the last except fire fighters to be there. Surely her stuff beneath the house was also crisped.

Putting her key in the lock of her own front
door, she remembered Mama's hours-ago "Don't
you dare." Taking a deep breath, she turned the
key, turned the knob, and pushed. Relief. The
chain lock was not on. Mama hadn't locked her
out.

2

The Jewelry Box

Nealy had fire engine dreams. Not huge, red, screaming, frightening, helping fire engines, but large toy ones, with functional parts such as removable ladders, extension ladders, and fire hoses with nozzles that really sprayed water. She dreamed she'd always wanted but never gotten a fine toy fire engine like that for Christmas. Not just for one Christmas, either, but for all her Christmases. She dreamed that she had wanted a fleet of fire engines and never gotten even one, so that every Christmas was a disappointment.

Even before she woke, even when she was still the person in the dream who wanted fire engines,

she knew she had never wanted a fire engine for
Christmas.

Mama's voice barked her awake.

"Ma'am?" As she cracked an eye she saw Mama
scowling from the doorway.

"Just look at yourself. Imagine crawling into
bed like that!"

Nealy looked. Black smears of soot streaked
both her and the sheets.

"I'm sorry," she said quickly. "I'll get everything clean."

"While you're at it, give both bathrooms the
toothbrush treatment," Mama said, giving morning orders. "And don't you be hanging around
that burned house, either."

"Yes, ma'am. No, ma'am," Nealy said, pulling
the sheet up around her neck. She wanted to pull
it over her head, to shut Mama out, but she didn't
dare. She knew that the main thing she wanted
to do was hang around the burned house, and
find a chance to go under it and check on her
stuff.

"How about starting right now?" Mama said,
waiting for Nealy to move.

Nealy jumped out of the bed and began stripping it.

"Just don't give me any grief, all right?" Mama said.

"No, ma'am," she said, rolling the sheets around her arms.

Without warning, Mama slapped her, a strong open palm against the cheek. It knocked her onto the bed. Mama waggled a finger in her face and said, "And you watch that mouth, young lady."

Inside her head she popped out with "What did I say?" but her best-girl mouth said, "Yes, Mama. I will."

"You get those bathrooms clean before you leave this house, do you hear me?"

Nealy opened her mouth one more time, to say "Yes, ma'am" but Mama cut her off, saying, "Don't you give me any lip," and stalked out of the house. There was no guessing when Mama would strike out.

Face stinging, she stepped to the mirror and saw her soot-smeared face with the whites of her eyes shining out. Beneath the soot, Mama's red handprint showed. You kept things clean in Mama's house. She knew that. But it was Noel Anne who gave lip, not her. Mama knew that. Wasn't it Mama who called Nealy best girl? The unbest girl no longer lived with them. Mama had kicked her out.

After stripping herself, she stuffed clothes and sheets into the washing machine. She remembered not to turn the machine on until after her shower. The city of Hanover had crummy water pressure. If she turned on the washing machine, she'd have an alternately hot and cold shower. They sure had power from the fire hydrants, though. Thank goodness.

Out of the shower, she ran to start the washer. Only after it hissed with filling did she scoot to do what she'd wanted to do from the instant she woke up. She ran to the living room and looked out the window.

It was true. Mrs. Dees's house had really burned. It stood dark and eyeless. Inside, beyond the large glassless windows, the house was as black as midnight. Some of the window frames were charred, and yesterday's window-high azaleas were dark, shriveled, and half the height. The break in the lattice where Nealy always ducked through to go under the house was openly visible.

It was also true about Noel Anne, and Nealy was part of the cause. Not all of it. Not even the main part of it. She didn't know why Noel Anne wanted to make so much trouble when there was enough already. Noel Anne was fourteen, boy-crazy, and independent, sneaking around dating when Mama forbade it. "You're too young," Mama would say, and Noel Anne would say back, "But you were dating even younger than this." Not knowing it was going to be thrown back at her, Mama had told them about how she had dated from the time she was twelve. She and Daddy had started dating when they were fourteen. Sure. And look how that turned out.

Nealy dragged a clean shirt and jeans onto her damp body, and as she ran out she jumped up and swung the crystal hanging by a string from the ceiling. Rainbows danced around the room.

Outside a mockingbird shrieked and dived at the Lyles' Siamese cat, which was lounging in the driveway. Nealy shrieked back at the bird, hissed at the cat, and hooked a finger under the collar of the Kennedys' cocker, who was about to charge at the cat. It was a dog-chase-cat, cat-eat-bird world. Waddling and sweet-talking Taffy, she dragged him to his yard at the corner before she crossed to Mrs. Dees's.

"You stay," she said, pointing a stern finger at the dog's nose.

Except for her and the mockingbird, the street was quiet, up and down. Mrs. Dees's car was not back yet. Nealy wondered if she even knew what had happened. Did anyone know where she'd gone, how to get in touch with her? Bright yellow tape surrounded the house and part of the yard. Black letters repeated themselves along the tape: DANGER FIRE LINE DO NOT CROSS.

Nealy longed to step over the tape and slip under the house to check on her things: her books, her drawing tablet, the jewelry box. Instead she strolled toward the front, staying outside the FIRE LINE DO NOT CROSS tape. Around all four front windows, the exterior wood was charred, and fire had roared out and destroyed the porch ceiling. Black chunks of what had been furniture were piled on the porch and even down on the sidewalk. The front door, amazingly enough, looked undamaged, and the whale door knocker, though no longer bright and brassy, still decorated the light wood.

Numbed by what had happened here, she idly put a hand onto the huge live oak in Mrs. Dees's yard. The bark of the tree pressed into her palm and, feeling it, she looked up. She hadn't even thought about this magnificent tree, which filled half of the world of Mrs. Dees's yard and towered above the house. Poor tree. She imagined it terrified of the fire and unable to move itself away. As she looked, however, the tree stood as always, appearing to be undamaged except for two small, twiggy branches, close to the porch, that had shriveled. A miracle.

On the roof, a sheet of plywood covered the place where the fire had burned through. A million questions whirled in her head. When had the plywood been put up? How had the fire started? Where would Mrs. Dees move to now? Had anyone else noticed the miracle of the tree? She looked around to find someone to ask, but both the front and side streets were as empty as though summer were over. Day care and day camp had swallowed all the kids. There was no sign of the crowd of last night.

Strolling back along the side of the house, she looked across the narrow twelve-foot width of the side yard. No glass in any window. No sign of curtains, just blackened walls and wires hanging from the ceiling. Lower, she examined the azaleas. They were shriveled, as though they had not so much been burned but had recoiled from the heat. The broken lattice, the secret door to her kingdom beneath the house, was no longer shielded from view.

Walking backward, as she often did, she checked the street again. No one. She looked south and checked for the bossy brats who thought they owned the world. No one. After one more glance, she pressed the tape down, stepped over it, and ducked under the house. Haunches high, she scrambled on hands and feet to the center support and turned quickly to be sure she could not be seen.

What she saw was a pale trail. The area beneath the house was blanketed with black except for the natural, light soil that revealed her scramble through the soot. She looked at herself. Knees black. Hands black. Clothes black. Soot had puffed up all over her. Looking up at the underside of the house, she saw no sign of the fire except for this soot, which had seeped down through the floorboards. Her box of things was also layered with soot. The sandhill cranes on the enameled jewelry box had disappeared beneath soot. Tentatively, she touched the box with one finger. The soot smeared like grease. When she blew it, soot whiffed up. Her eyes sealed themselves shut and spared themselves as she got a faceful. Thank goodness for reflexes, she thought. But her guilt reflex had popped open as fast as her eyes had slammed shut.

When she'd taken the jewelry box from Mama's dresser, she hadn't felt guilty at all. It had been Grandma's, the only thing Mama had kept when Grandma was killed in a car accident two years ago. Nealy and Noel Anne had both wanted some of Grandma's things, but Mama hadn't wanted memories, as if her mind wouldn't keep them anyway. Her mind had kept memories of her brothers. Noel Anne and Nealy were named after Mama's twin brothers, killed in the Vietnam War.

With Daddy gone and Noel Anne more rambunctious than Mama could stand, Nealy had felt a need for Grandma, who had held steady no matter what. She wanted the jewelry box, needed it, thought it should be hers, so she'd taken it and added it to her stash beneath Mrs. Dees's house. Then Mama had accused Noel Anne. Nealy had tried to confess, but Mama thought Nealy was just trying to take sides with Noel Anne and wouldn't listen. Now Noel Anne was gone and the box was ruined.

With sad pleasure, she noticed that, with her blowing, the edges of the cranes were visible behind a gray film. She had planned to return the box to her mother's dresser and make her listen. Now she'd have to try to get it clean first. The word *clean* made her laugh. She looked like a chimney sweep. Now the word reminded her that she'd left the clothes in the washer. One of Mama's rules was never to let washed clothes stay wadded in the washer or dried clothes stay wrinkling in the dryer.

Without much energy or joy, she scooted back across on the same pale trail she'd made coming under. If anyone noticed, maybe they'd think an animal had been there. She'd often pretended to be an animal under here when Mrs. Dees had heard her and stomped on the floor saying, "Git! Git!"

The azalea hedge was no longer a shield, and she was totally exposed as she emerged from under the house. Pushing the tape down, she stepped across it and into the street, trying, as always, to look as though all she had been doing was walking down the street.

As quickly as she could, while still appearing casual to any observer, she strolled across to her house and in. Before she knew it, she had made black tracks on the carpet. *Sheesh.* She reopened the door and yanked off her socks and shoes. Then back to the shower, dumping her clothes on the floor. Then clean, and again naked, she padded to the washer and put the clean clothes from the washer into the dryer. Returning to the bathroom, she brought her sooty clothes to the washer. Then she slipped into shorts and a T-shirt, retrieved her socks and sneakers and added them and soap powder to the load, and turned on both machines.

Now her hands were sooty again. While the clothes washed and dried, she cleaned the three black footprints off the carpet. For the first time in her life, she appreciated Mama's lectures on cleaning. She found some Carpet Kleen under the kitchen sink and got to it. Even so, all she did at first was smear soot. But every reapplication and scrubbing took out a little more soot until finally the carpet was clean and avocado green again. Then she violated Mama's bedroom space and borrowed the hair dryer. She felt like a professional rug cleaner drying the rug this way. Maybe she could add this to her money-earning skills.

Folding the clothes and putting them away

made her remember that Noel Anne had split without any clothes. Gathering a few things from her sister's room, she stuffed them into her blue-and-yellow book bag. She huffed a sigh. She'd been cleaning things all morning and hadn't even done the bathrooms yet. Well, one of them was partly done just from cleaning up the soot. But hunger and Noel Anne called more strongly than bathrooms. She could get to them this afternoon before Mama came home from work.

In the kitchen she threw together a thick sprouts, tomato, and onion sandwich. Then she hitched the book bag over her shoulders, chomped on the sandwich, and reached up and swung the crystal as she headed out. She left with rainbows dancing in the room.

3
Noel Anne

At least Nealy knew where to find Noel Anne. Finished with its snooze in the sun, the Lyles' cat was stalking a squirrel. Both cat and squirrel twitched their tails. Nealy meowed at the cat and clucked to the squirrel.

At the corner, an earsplitting snarl of machinery drew her attention away from Noel Anne and Mama, cat and squirrel. Down Dartmouth Street, trucks and barricades blocked the street. It took a walking moment for her to comprehend, then she ran, book bag thudding at her back. Saws ripped away at the three-hundred-year-old live oak. The one in the middle of the street where the road split and went around.

"What's going on?" she yelled as she ran. The area was surrounded by bright yellow tape imprinted again and again around its length: DANGER PEOPLE AT WORK DO NOT CROSS. The thunder of machinery chewed up the sound of her voice, so she reached across the yellow tape and yanked at the shirt of one of the hard-hatted workers.

"Struck by lightning," he said, barely glancing over his shoulder as he waved directions to men in a bucket raised up into the tree. Already fat limbs had been shorn and lowered to the ground, then sliced into enormous logs. A machine with crablike claws grabbed the logs and loaded them onto a truck. The machinery sounded as though it were eating up the world.

"There are baby squirrels!" she shouted, pointing to the very limb now having the saw put to it. There had been four baby squirrels in a hole in the tree, newborn and hairless, all head with closed, bulging eyes. Frantically, she yanked on the man's shirt again. He didn't even look around. She understood that he was busy, but the squirrels! The tree! She looked around for help, but there was only the work crew and a couple of kids who were delighted with the action.

In a nearby tree she spotted two fat squirrels,

mouths moving in protest, though she couldn't hear them for the noise. She knew they were clucking, scolding. Their home was being demolished and maybe their babies, too. Could squirrels move their young out of danger the way cats did? She almost cried for those homeless squirrels. She shifted the book bag containing the clothes for Noel Anne. She couldn't imagine how anything, animals or people, could manage if they didn't have a place called home.

Lightning, huh? she thought, and she realized the futility of stopping them and walked away. This tree had not been damaged two days ago when she'd climbed it and discovered the baby squirrels. There had been no rain for weeks. No rain, no thunder, no lightning. The daily news was full of drought and parched Georgia earth. The limb where the nest had been was now just an empty space against the sky. Spanish moss lay in piles, like wiry gray hair yanked from thousands of heads.

"Lightning!" she shouted back toward them, unheard. "There hasn't been any lightning!" She stalked off down King Street. Why were they taking down a perfectly beautiful tree? The sides of the trucks were lettered CITY OF HANOVER. Her city was doing this? The city she treasured and traipsed all over?

By the time she got to town, she was irritated with Noel Anne as well as with the city. Why did people cause trouble by doing stupid things? She turned on Princess Street, angled across Grand Square, and shoved into the Yogurt Shoppe. "Shoppay," she thought with a snort. Too cutesy for her.

"I brought you some things," she said, practically slamming the book bag down on a table.

"I guess you want a freebie," Noel Anne said, her sugary voice and a smile disguising the warning glance. Noel Anne's warning glance meant for her to act as if she had merely come for yogurt and not to dare act like a sister.

"No," said Nealy, identically pleasant, dragging the book bag to the counter. "I just brought you some things." One of the things Noel Anne had done to upset Mama was to lie about her age to get this job. Mama had not marched to the Yogurt Shoppe in a steam of anger, however, to expose Noel Anne and make her lose the job.

"What flavor do you want?" Noel Anne asked, almost gritting her teeth behind her smile.

"Strawberry," Nealy said from behind her own

frozen-yogurt smile. "Small. With lots of sprin-kles." Making a big display of fishing for her money, she brought it forth and handed it to Noel Anne. She didn't even like yogurt, but she was no freebie-mooching sister. Taking the napkin-wrapped cone, she plunked the book bag to the floor at the end of the counter.

"Thanks," Noel Anne said. "Come back soon." Still the huge smile, still clerk to customer, but meaning *get out of here fast.*

Behind her Nealy heard the door open. When she looked, it was the old customers going out and no new customers coming in.

"How are you?" she whispered, leaning toward Noel Anne.

"Oh, fine," Noel Anne said, making her face reflect all the fineness. "It's just been two days."

"Isn't it scary?" Nealy still whispered.

"Scary? No." The "fine" face hid any scared-ness.

"Are you with Daddy?" Even as she asked the question, assuming the answer, she was a little envious of Noel Anne being with Daddy.

"Hah!" said Noel Anne. "What do you think? Do you think he wants me around with his precious Marlene?" With a cleaning cloth, Noel Anne took a hard swipe at the steel cabinets.

Nealy mashed three fingers against her lips. "I just thought . . ." She couldn't yet imagine being on her own when she was grown, much less fourteen. "It would scare me to death."

"I know it would. That's because you're such a little scaredy slavey chicken, anyhow."

"No, I'm not," Nealy protested. "I just try to get along with Mama."

"Mama's crazy," Noel Anne said.

Nealy almost jumped at the statement of a perhaps-truth. But she was only eleven years old and Grandma was dead and Daddy didn't want her. What else was she supposed to do except try to get along with Mama?

"I miss you," she said to Noel Anne.

"Oh, Mary Neal, pleeeease!" and on the end of her *please* the door wheezed open and there were customers. "Git," Noel Anne hissed.

Nealy got. She was good at that, at becoming as invisible as possible to anyone who might cause her trouble. Never mind that she would have asked if there was anything else Noel Anne wanted. Never mind that she was sure she had seen a glint in Noel Anne's eyes when Nealy had said she missed her. Nealy got. Once she was outside, she tossed the yogurt cone head first into the trash.

So, what did you want? she asked herself as she wandered on automatic pilot to the Queen Street Book Shop. Did you want her to bow down and kiss your feet in thanks? Yes, she had. Some show of appreciation would have been very nice. Why did some sisters feel obligated to hate each other? In front of the glass window of the bookstore, she stared not into the store but into herself. From books she'd read about times past, she knew that some people never had a home with a mother and a father and everyone in the same house, all getting along fine. She knew this. So why, with crime and drugs and homeless people on the television news every day, why did it feel like only her? Why did it feel like only her family was in disarray? She missed Grandma, who had seemed to get through life smoothly, no matter what.

She blinked, saw books, and walked into the book shop, _s-h-o-p._ No _shoppay_ here.

"Well, Nealy, what are you after today?" Mrs. Frazier said, friendly, ready to help. Now that seemed like a good family. Mr. and Mrs. Frazier, Laura Catherine, Mark, and Alex.

"Oh, just looking," she said. "I hope to be able to buy the butterfly book soon." However erratic Mama could be, she was fair about money, and Nealy was diligent about earning any extra money Mama offered by doing yard work or extra cleaning.

With her index and middle fingers, she slid *Field Guide to North American Butterflies* off the shelf. Just holding it bathed her spirit in butterflies. These insects looked so fragile, yet had more methods of defense than most creatures. One was the eye spots at the ends of their wings, which drew the attention of birds and lizards away from their vital body parts. Also, they blended with their environment, and some of them resembled toxic objects, so predators avoided them. And they could fly incredible distances during migration. Wouldn't that be marvelous, she thought, to be able to fly away? She shrugged. Wishfully, she returned the book to the shelf, walked out of the store, and crossed to go home.

4

Mama

With her thoughts of Noel Anne and families and
flying away, Nealy had forgotten the tree until she
was in hearing range of the machinery. In just
those few minutes, the tree was nearly down.

Trucks were hauling off enormous chunks of
tree, and one truck was being fed leaves and
smaller branches. With a loud, zipping buzz, the
machine chewed them up and spit them into the
interior.

Wood chips, Nealy thought. The machine was
making wood chips. She loved wood chips. Her
driveway was covered with them. Not only did
they smell good, but they made a no-skinned-
knees sort of driveway. Splinters, maybe, but no

skinned knees. One of the extra jobs Mama paid her for was keeping the wood chips raked into the driveway instead of scattered in the yard. She'd never thought of them being made from live trees. In fact, she hadn't thought of them at all, but she would have thought they were made from trees already dead, like the insects she collected. Trees really struck by lightning, perhaps. Not trees that were killed for them.

When she turned away, she fled to Mama, hustling back down Dartmouth Street to and beyond the wooden bridge that straddled the marsh and tidal canal. At the highway, she checked traffic carefully before she darted across to Mama's office. When she pushed through the doorway of the Department of Natural Resources, the receptionist beamed at her, friendly as always.

When she reached Mama's office, Mama frowned. "Mary Neal, what are you doing here?"

Why was she always surprised at Mama's reaction? Why did she always expect Mama to be nice? Like the receptionist. Like Mrs. Frazier at the bookstore. Like Grandma.

"Somebody's cutting down a tree, that live oak in the middle of Dartmouth Street down from the house, they said it got hit by lightning but it didn't, there hasn't been any lightning, and there was a nest of baby squirrels and—"

"Whoa," Mama said. "Who-body? What tree? Where have you been?"

"The tree in the middle of Dartmouth Street," Nealy said. "I don't know who-body. The City of Hanover, I guess." Hands waving, she rattled on again, describing the machinery and the taking-down and chopping-up and the man who wouldn't listen and the baby squirrels.

"You didn't bring home any squirrels!" This was not a question, it was a statement. An exclamation against.

"No. It was too late."

"Thank goodness." Mama spoke with more firmness than thanks. "Where have you been and why did you leave the house before doing your chores?"

Mama had her. How did Mama know?

Mama reached across the desk to hand Nealy something. A key. "Here. And I want you to get home and get those bathrooms done. And for not doing it before, you can also clean the utility room."

Nealy opened her mouth and shut it. The utility

room was usually an extra job, for pay. She saw
the butterfly field guide fluttering off into the distance. Reaching into her pocket, she pulled out
her key. "I have my key." What did Mama think,
that she went around losing her key?

"I went home at lunch and changed the locks,"
Mama said, still holding out the key.

"Changed the locks?"

"To keep Noel Anne out."

As far as Nealy knew, Noel Anne hadn't tried
to get back in.

"And don't you dare let her in. I left you a note
on the door."

Nealy thought she might melt down or explode. Mama and her "don't you dares." Why
didn't she go find Noel Anne and bring her home?
She wasn't hard to find. Why didn't Mama care?
About trees, about squirrels, about Noel Anne?
Mama was the one who was supposed to care.
She was the one, she and Grandma, who had
taught Nealy to care about the earth and all its
creatures. It was even Mama's job, taking care of
the earth. Nealy had grown up with Mama bringing her down here to see whatever was in the
small aquarium. A ridley turtle, or some strange

mollusk. The nameplate on Mama's desk read MARILYN COMPTON. Who was this Marilyn Compton?

"Marilyn Compton, don't you care?" Nealy was smugly pleased with her play on words: Don't you *dare*. Don't you *care*?

Mama gave her a hard look. "I have reached my limit on caring."

Nealy shifted her position, trying to feel strong and sturdy. "I didn't know there was a limit." Mama certainly wasn't like her own mother. Grandma had never reached the end of caring and she would let you talk about anything.

"Mamaaaaa," Nealy wailed, frustrated and sad. "Noel Anne should be home."

Mama half stood, reached over, and plucked Nealy's sticky T-shirt away from her chest. "You're a mess."

Nealy hunched a shoulder, surprised only that it had taken Mama so long to say it. She wanted so much to say, "Who cares?" but that was a dangerous, Noel Anne response, and she was the best girl. Instead, she plowed her hand through her thick, dark, sweaty hair. From a pocket she took a barrette and shoved her hair up and clipped it.

Mama shook her head and frowned.

Noel Anne was cute and pretty, and one of the reasons she acted out was to keep from being Mama's little doll. So Mama tried to force it on Nealy. Fat chance. True, she looked a lot like both of them, with good skin and thick, softly curly hair that looked good no matter what they did with it. But she wasn't going to be Mama's doll, either. She smoothed the front of her shirt until it stuck back to her hot body. "Who can I talk to about it?"

"About what?"

"The tree."

Mama's sharp reply was, "The mayor."

"Yeah, sure." Nealy took a deep breath and let it out with a long, cheek-puffing blow.

"Mary Neal, you look like a slovenly nerd."

To try to amuse herself Nealy thought, Mama used the *N* word. Raising her hand and making a waggle-fingered wave, she said, "Nerd leaving," and she walked out of Mama's office and out of the building without even stopping to check the aquarium.

Instead of tromping across the wooden bridge, she sat on it, vaguely wishing, wishing. Wishing what? That she could fly like the monarch? That she could at least have a nest in the marsh like the clapper rail she heard squawking? Her eyes roved the marsh to see if she could find the timid marsh hen. Her gaze combed the grasses as the bird called again and again. Nealy squawked back and demanded, "Let me see you." Their camouflage was perfect.

The tide was flowing. There was just a trickle now, but when the tide came in here it was already full at the beach. The water pushed inland, searching out its last places to go. When it came, it came quickly. This canal was a muddy slough at low tide and full enough for canoeing at high tide. If I had a canoe, she thought, wondering how long it would take to save enough money for a canoe.

The marsh hen was still squawking, and suddenly she saw the reason for the clapper rail's disturbance. Just below her, three black, fluffy clapper rail chicks stood on a marsh flat with water trickling around their feet.

"Go, you idiot kids!" she hollered at them, laughing. How unusual for the little ones not to respond to the mother's call. These were Noel Anne chicks.

Quietly, and so quickly that Nealy didn't see

her come, the marsh hen mom was next to the chicks. With five or six movements of her feet, she pulled down some fronds of marsh grass and made a high-ground sort of place. Standing on it, she chortled and fussed. One chick hopped right up, the second climbed up, and the third struggled up.

What a treat! This was the sort of thing Nealy could watch all day long. But the day was already more than half over and Mama's orders ruffled her contentment. She had to go. But she watched the marsh hen strike off in long-legged strides, calling her chicks. The hen disappeared into the tall grasses and reappeared, wading to a mud bank. One of the chicks immediately disappeared into the grass, came out, and swam across a small eddy to the mother. More slowly, the second chick did the same. The third chick clung to its perch, and gripping the railing of the bridge, Nealy clung to hers. She was intrigued by the behavior of the three, one who was active and able, one who wasn't quite sure, and one who couldn't manage at all. She knew she was like the first. And maybe Noel Anne was, too.

The hen took two lengthy steps into the water, starting back for the remaining chick, which was

fourteen feet away and out of her sight. The other
two plunged into the water after her. She clucked
at them as if to chase them back, but they stuck
close. The hen looked into the distance where
the lone chick was, then back at the two, as
though thinking about the choice of risking the
two to save the one. When the two would not
be left, she stepped back to the mud bank and
stayed with them.

The water was rising quickly. The mud flat
where they had stood minutes ago was already
awash, and the water was rising on the hen-made
hummock and the lone chick. How easily Nealy
could go around, pick up the slow chick, and put
it with the others. If she interfered, however, she
knew she would frighten the hen away, and instead of returning, the bird might very well aban-
don all three chicks.

After an interminable time, that third chick
flopped off the roost and disappeared into the
grass. The other two had zipped through the five-
or six-foot distance, but this one didn't emerge.
Nealy despaired for it, wishing, now, she had rescued it. She could take it home and keep it in a
box. She shrugged away what Mama would say
about that. Was the water too deep in the grasses?

How much harder now to find the chick even in that small amount of marsh grass.

Minutes and minutes and minutes passed as the mother hen chortled. At last the bedraggled chick appeared from the grasses and collapsed into the edge of the water, where it just lay. The mama moved with astonishing speed. With three wide strides, she crossed the eddy, picked the chick up by the head, and carried it to the mud bank.

Ahhhh. Nealy sighed with relief. Things like this were not in the field guides. She relaxed her grip on the railing, encouraged, and ready to go about Mama's business. If clapper rails could move their young, maybe gray squirrels could, too.

She called out, "Good job, Mom," and made her own long-legged strides for home. On the way she thought she might have time to go back under the house and still get those cleaning chores done.

But Mrs. Dees was home.

5
Soot

Apparently Mrs. Dees had just arrived.

People were gathered around her on the porch and straggling down the stairs to the yard. Nealy scooted up to join the crowd, nearly as breathless as she had been the night of the fire, wanting to tell Mrs. Dees how sorry she was about the fire. She wanted someone to say the same to her, but of course no one knew it was her house, too.

"It's like a death," someone on the porch was saying. "I can't imagine what it is like to lose everything."

"No," Mrs. Dees said sharply. "It is not like a death; it doesn't compare with the loss of human life. Thank goodness I was gone. Thank goodness

I had the cat with me. She never would have been able to get out. It *is* a terrible thing but, no, it's not like a death."

No one told her there had been a rumor that someone had died in the fire. A policeman drove up front and walked onto the porch. He and Mrs. Dees disappeared into the blackened house. Afraid the house would collapse on the two, almost everyone gasped, including Nealy.

"The house is sound," a man on the porch reassured them. Nealy immediately moved from the sidewalk to the porch, wanting more information.

"Isn't it dangerous for them to be in there?" she asked.

"No, no," said the man, who seemed to know. "It was a quick, hot fire that destroyed everything but didn't damage the structure of the house."

Nealy peered through the open, gaping windows. The house looked destroyed to her. Wires hung from ceilings and everything else was just murky black rubble on the floor. Mounds of ashes were unidentifiable.

Voices crossed and crisscrossed talking about it.

"I heard this strange sound and thought, well, Mrs. Dees is back, and what is she doing?" It was

Ms. Royster talking, Mrs. Dees's next-door neighbor. Everyone quieted to listen to this closest witness. "I opened my drapes and looked out and saw fire right in front of my face. I couldn't believe it was really happening," Ms. Royster continued. "I yanked the drapes shut and just stood there, not believing. Then I opened them again and it was really fire! I was just going to the back to wash my clothes, so I grabbed up the laundry basket and the car keys and headed for the door."

Someone laughed. "Hey! If your house caught fire, too, you were at least going to have some clothes."

"I was afraid the tree or moss would catch fire and fall on my roof," Ms. Royster said.

"Yes. These old houses are so close together."

"The wood in oak trees is so dense it's hard for them to catch fire," Nealy said, but no one heard. They were still concentrating on Ms. Royster.

"Didn't you call the fire department?" someone else asked. "I was going to. I was heading to the phone on the way to the door, but I heard the sirens."

"Us, too," Nealy said, including herself in her

mother's action when actually she had been at the window, paralyzed. Mama had instantly thought what to do. Nealy thought of these three women, Mama, Ms. Royster, and Mrs. Dees, right here together in the neighborhood, the lone adult in each house.

"Who called?"

"We did," said a neighbor from across the street and several doors down. "We heard the *poof* noises, too, and looked out. There was a boy standing in the street in front of our house, staring back. He was watching the house and the house was on fire, and the boy ran."

"Arson," someone said, and others murmured agreement.

"I heard they found a body in the house."

"No," Nealy said. "There was no body."

They paid her less attention than if she'd been a gnat, and they kept on buzzing about the body.

"The flames were leaping up through the roof," someone said.

"No, no," said the man who knew the structure was sound. "They chopped a hole in the roof to vent the fire, but no flames leaped through the roof."

Nealy moved closer to him. She thought that

he and she had the truest facts about the fire instead of starting dramatic rumors.

"What do you mean, vent the fire?"

"The heat is powerful," he said. "It blew the windows out. That's what made the *poof* sounds we all heard. That pressure can even explode a house. The first thing they do is try to chop holes, preferably at some high point, to let out some of the heat so it will be safe to go in and fight the fire."

There was a sudden silence as Mrs. Dees and the police officer returned from the tour of the house. Mrs. Dees looked out and up.

"I'm so glad it didn't hurt the tree," she said. "When I heard about it, the first thing I thought was how lucky no one was here and I had the cat with me. The second thing I thought was, ohhhh, the poor tree."

Everyone murmured relief about Mrs. Dees's safety, if not for the cat or the tree.

"I pictured it drawing its limbs to its trunk and wanting to scream because it couldn't get away from the flames," Mrs. Dees said.

Nealy nodded, having seen that image herself, and she smiled at Mrs. Dees for caring so much about the tree.

"Mrs. Dees," the police officer said, "I know how difficult this is, but I really need to know if anything is missing."

Mrs. Dees gave a half-laugh, half-cry and swept her arm to indicate the charred remains of her house. "Everything is missing."

The officer looked earnest and sympathetic. "We might not be able to prove it, but we know it was arson and usually there is a burglary connected with arson. If you could think of some particular thing, something metal—a bicycle or the television . . ."

"What would that prove?" Mrs. Dees asked.

"We could locate the remains of something metal. If there are none, we can assume that item was stolen. For instance, I don't see any debris in the living room that looks like it would have been the TV."

"The television is—uh, was in the den. My bicycle was in the dining room." The two disappeared again into the somber house, surrounded by soot.

As the people on the porch began talking again, Nealy moved to the left and looked in the window. Mrs. Dees and the police officer were pushing at the rubble with their shoes.

"Hmph," said Mrs. Dees, toeing a round mound of ashes. "That was my dining room table. But I don't see anything that looks like meltdown of bicycle."

"Ah," the police officer said. "Can you describe it for me? Do you have the serial number?"

Mrs. Dees gave another harsh laugh. "La, I have no idea where the serial number is. I've had that bike for years. It's bright light blue, a five-speed Schwinn." Then a lighter laugh. "It had a sticker on the back fender that said HAVE YOU HUGGED YOUR BIKE TODAY?" She patted the air where the fender would have been.

Nealy smiled to herself. She knew that sticker.

"Anything else? When did you buy it? And where?"

Mrs. Dees shook her head. "I have no idea when," she said, but she named a bike shop.

"Anything else? How about the TV?" With that Mrs. Dees led the way from one black room to another, and they disappeared.

Nealy turned to the porch murmurers. "Her bike is missing," she announced, pleased to add a bit of information. "There was no metal meltdown that would have been her bike."

Now the talk turned to Mrs. Dees and her bike, how she used to roll it across the porch and lift it down the stairs and pedal around town on her errands.

Back on the porch, Mrs. Dees and the officer revealed that there was no meltdown of television, either. And a large ceramic clown she had made was gone from a table that was still standing in the back hall. There were no shards of clown in the surrounding debris. Mrs. Dees brushed her hands together, then held them out to show that the soot just stuck and smeared. Nealy had discovered that, too.

Mrs. Dees stared out off the porch to the street, as if she could see her bike or her television or her house as whole and entire as they had been when she'd left two days before.

"What will you do?" someone asked. "Do you have a place to go?"

"I have no idea what I'll do," she said, staring into space and looking defeated. "Fortunately I do have a friend who has a rental house a few blocks away, and the downstairs tenant there has just moved. So not only do I have a place to go, I have a familiar place to go. I was with my friend when he bought the house several years ago and sat with him many an hour while he worked on restoring it."

"Will you renovate your house?"

Mrs. Dees shrugged and looked around. "I have no idea. They say it's sound, that the structure is sound." She held out her black hands again. "I don't know." Then, as if coming out of a dream, Mrs. Dees looked around the porch, as though just now seeing this gathering of people.

Her eyes lit and stuck on Nealy. They seemed to Nealy to be accusing eyes. Did Mrs. Dees think she was the boy seen in the street? She almost said, "I'm a girl," and she did pat her chest as though her eleven-year-old still-flat chest would prove something. In her attempt to be the opposite of Noel Anne, she wore jeans and boys' shirts.

"I don't mean to be rude," Mrs. Dees said, "but I really don't want anyone around right now unless it's someone I know."

Nealy looked up. There were several people Nealy didn't know among the curious, the concerned, the comforting.

"It's just that I don't know who did this. I don't

mean I think you did it, but I just want you to
please go."

There were a few shuffling steps but no one
made a move to leave. There were choruses of,
"If there's anything I can do to help, please let
me know." There were kids from the neighborhood, four of Nealy's antagonists. But as mean as
they were to her, she couldn't imagine them starting a fire. She realized Mrs. Dees was still looking
at her.

"Me?" Nealy said in surprise, hand to her chest
again, looking to see if Mrs. Dees meant someone
else. Everyone else was looking at her, too, shaking their heads in sympathy or suspicion.

"But I . . ." Nealy started.

"Mama," said Mrs. Dees's daughter, Adriana,
who used to babysit for Noel Anne and Nealy,
"you know it wasn't Nealy."

"Please go now," Mrs. Dees said, looking at
Nealy as though she'd never seen her before.

Nealy was glad of her dark complexion because
it didn't show the red of her blush. If only she
could become instantly invisible and get off this
porch without having to move through the
crowd, without having to walk past Mrs. Dees.

She wanted to say, "Don't you know it's my house, too? Don't you know that when you stomp on the floor and say 'Git,' it's me?"

The railing on the street end of the house had burned, along with the azaleas behind it. As though it were a normal way to leave the porch, she turned and stepped to that end of the porch and leaped out over the charred azaleas. A cloud of soot puffed up as she landed, and she stepped quickly into Amherst Street and gave a casual half-wave back to the people on the porch. No one but Mrs. Dees was even looking.

As she dallied across the street she heard their voices, louder than they thought. Mrs. Dees, or was it Adriana, was telling how even as a tot, Nealy had wandered the street and when she needed to pee, she'd just squat wherever she was. They thought she didn't hear them. Maybe they thought she didn't remember. She had been young then, but she remembered. The need to steer clear of Mama had been with her even then.

What she hadn't known was that so many eyes had been watching. How had she ever thought that no one knew she sneaked beneath Mrs. Dees's house? Mrs. Dees probably knew exactly who was underneath the house when she stomped her foot and said "Git!"

Now they thought she was the "boy" who had set the fire. Mrs. Dees thought it was her!

To keep from running home as if she were guilty, she changed direction and walked south on Amherst, near the azalea hedge bordering Mrs. Dees's backyard. She examined the shrubbery for bugs. There was only an ant, not on the azaleas but crawling up a very small twig that arched so it touched the ground only at the stem and tip. Some people said ants were smart, but she'd watched ants for jillions of hours and hadn't seen a smart one yet. Hard-working, maybe. But stupid. This creature scurried like crazy over every millimeter of the slender stick once, twice, three times. Finding nothing of special interest, it started off and did not seem to know how to get down or how it had gotten up in the first place. Nealy didn't know how she'd gotten to the place she was in, either, so what did that make her? And if she was standing here watching an ant one more time, she must be as stupid as the ant.

Now Mike and Bobby and Josh and Lisa whizzed past her. "You can't come down our street," Bobby said. She ignored them, and they ran to the huge live oak in front of Bobby's house and scrambled into it.

"Six, five, four, three. Stay away from our tree," the four of them chanted as she continued her walk.

"Are you deaf, Creature Freak?" This was Josh. His deep, marbley voice was easy to identify.

Now Lisa called out, "Fee, fie, foe, fum. This is where you should not come." If they had noticed Mrs. Dees's accusation, they hadn't started on that yet. She was sorry she'd thought they couldn't have done it. Maybe they could have.

Suddenly she was pelted by their arsenal of acorns. The first ones made her flinch, but she didn't cry out or hop around. She would never let them make her jump or dance or run. Still, when hurled from strong arms, they stung, these tiniest of acorns which grew into these hugest of trees. Without changing her direction or pace, she looked up at the boys and the one traitor girl.

"Did you see they took down the tree on Dartmouth Street?" she asked, putting up an arm to protect her eyes from the persistent assault.

"Who cares?" Lisa peppered Nealy with a handful of small missiles. Lisa ought to be her friend,

Nealy thought. They were both girls, and they both liked to climb trees.

"You'd better care," she said, still shielding her eyes. "They're going to cut down your tree, too." She didn't know why they'd taken down the other tree, but it sounded like a good threat.

"Sure they are, Freak," Mike said. "You'd be the first to know about it."

"Yeah," said Josh. "You'd be the first to know, since you're going to grow up and marry a tree."

"Or a bug," Bobby cracked. "Yeah, bugs and trees are going to be your relatives."

Acorns and laughter fell on her head.

"The city is taking out all the trees that interfere with the street, you stupid jerks!" She stomped the words with her tongue but her feet walked slowly, quietly as she turned away, heading for home. She wanted to shout back, "Who cares?" But she knew who cared. She did.

At the edge of the yard next to Bobby's, a ladybug was crawling on the blue blossom of a hydrangea bush. A two-dotted ladybug. Sticking out a finger, she coaxed the insect onto it and let it crawl for a minute. Mama and Grandma said ladybugs used to have lots of polka dots but that something was happening in the environment to cause them to lose their dots. Yeah, she thought. People were as stupid as ants, not being careful about the earth and the air.

"Ladybug, ladybug, fly away home!" the four shouted from the tree, barraging her again. "Your house is on *fire!*" They giggled at this, and the real ladybug flew.

Nealy glanced up Amherst to the back of the burned house. She squared her shoulders and walked slowly home.

6

Solace

Later, when the police, fire, and insurance investigators, the curious and the concerned, as well as Mrs. Dees, had left, Nealy crossed the yellow fire-line tape and crawled back under the house.

Soot had drifted through the floorboards and covered her path. Her things were even thicker with soot but this time, she had brought supplies.

Cool. It was always cool here, even in hot summer and even with the house above gutted by fire. Heat rose and cool air fell, and with the oak tree shading the house, the cool air was trapped under here. She needed this, the seclusion and the coolness. At her house, even with no one else there, she could feel Mama everywhere. Inside the clean and tidy cabinets and closets, inside her own impeccable closet, Mama was there. This place, under Mrs. Dees's house, was hers. Even with the soot below and the destruction above, this place was hers alone.

Tenderly she lifted the jewelry box out of the sooty cardboard box. As she wiped with paper towels, the cranes gradually emerged from beneath the veil of soot. With a combination of spit and rubbing, she polished the lacquered box. Grandma's box. Mama's box. Nealy's box. As she had done so many times before, she rubbed it, stroking her hand across the glassy surface as though the box were Aladdin's lamp and something magic, if not a genie, would pop out.

As if in a dream, she saw herself standing in the doorway of Mama's room, her eyes moving like magnets to this white enameled jewelry box. She was sorry this had caused an upset, with Mama accusing Noel Anne and not listening when she, Nealy, had tried to tell the truth.

"Don't you stick up for your sister!" Mama had roared, too angry to hear Nealy's confession. "I have enough trouble without you starting."

"But Mama, I—"

"No, Nealy, no." Mama had rolled right over

her. "Don't stick up for that rotten kid." In a surprise gesture, Mama had pulled Nealy close, hugged her, and rubbed the back of her head.

Nealy had frozen at the unaccustomed hug, but she had liked it. She had wanted to lean into it and keep it forever. "You are my best girl. I couldn't stand it if you turned out like Noel Anne."

Nealy had gasped. Here she'd tried so hard not to be like her sister and was like her anyway, in the worst ways. But she reminded herself that this was just one of many problems between Mama and Noel Anne, and she had not caused the others. And sitting here in soot beneath Mrs. Dees's house, she had to admit she felt good about having the box. She didn't let herself think of the words Mama had thrown at Noel Anne: *stolen, thief.* There was only pleasure in having it, as if the box were Grandma herself. Rubbing her hand across the smooth white surface, tracing the outlines of the four tall sandhill cranes, she realized that what she really wanted was to have Grandma float out of the box. Essence of Grandma.

Lifting the lid, she listened to the tune. The name of the song, listed on the bottom of the box, was "The Way We Were." Grandma, who'd had this jewelry box as long as Nealy could remember, had told her that the song was about memories of "the way we were." Memories of Grandma floated out along with the music, and Nealy ached for her, for something warm and loving and unchanging. She willed Grandma to speak to her, to advise her, but Grandma no more spoke up than God ever did.

What spoke was the music, louder than Big Ben. She slammed the box shut and looked around fearfully. What did she think she was doing, announcing her presence to all the world? Heat surged to her face, like it had to Mama's handprint this morning. Was it only this morning? Had the fire been only last night? It seemed like days.

She put her finger on the stem of the music release and opened the box. There was no ghost of Grandma here, only the insect collection, placed in this velvet-lined box only two days ago. To her amazement, she saw that soot had even gotten inside this box!

One by one, she lifted the insects, the fat blue-green June bug first. She blew on it and even wiped it gently, then set it temporarily in the clean cardboard box she'd brought. With careful blowing, the black praying mantis returned to green, though a darker green than before, and wiping was not too successful.

The soot didn't blow off the tiger swallowtails, whose fragile wings couldn't be wiped at all. She had been so proud to have one in the dark phase and one in the tiger-striped phase. Now they were both black. Their gorgeous border colors were lost beneath soot. Even so, she was not ready to give them up, so she spread a paper towel in the box and set them on it. She might never have either one again, much less both, because she didn't catch and kill, but collected only those she found already dead.

Soot didn't blow off the blue velvet lining, either. But she would return later with Mama's rug cleaner. Without even intending it, she had become an expert in cleaning soot. When she was finished, she set the insects back onto the still-sooty lining and placed the jewelry box in the clean cardboard box.

Remembering how gorgeous her drawings had looked, she reached next for her large drawing pad. Using paper towels to cover her sooty fingers, she peeked in at her last drawing. Satisfaction rippled through her. The inside of the sketchbook was clean and her drawing of the insects in the jewelry box was even better than she remembered. When she had moved the mirrored lid, she could see insects twice, and she had drawn them twice, once just as they lay on velvet and again using both the reality and the reflection.

She wiped the cover and sides of her small sketch pad without looking inside and turned her attention to her field guides. They, too, were clean inside and sooty only on the covers and the edges. The covers wiped nicely clean. Again, spit helped. But the edges, she thought, would be permanently gray. As she cleaned the *Field Guide to the Mammals* she thought about the squirrels, and as she cleaned the *Field Guide to the Trees of North America* she opened it and read again about the live oaks. She loved these guidebooks. They were the main thing she spent her money on. Her first one, *A Field Guide to the Birds,* had been a gift from Grandma after their trip to the Okefenokee Swamp, where they'd seen the sandhill cranes, like the cranes on Grandma's jewelry box. She also had field guides to the reptiles and amphibians, the insects and the shells and the wildflowers. And there were more. Butterflies would be next.

When everything was as clean as she could get it and put in the fresh box, Nealy covered the box with an old shirt she'd brought to keep out the soot.

Probably she should bring everything with her. If she was caught under the house now, she would really be in trouble. But this was her place, too. If she removed her things, it would be like losing her claim, which was utterly stupid, she knew. She had no claim. Just the same, leaving the small sketchbook and everything but the large one, she crawled out, sooty once more.

Immediately, she was alarmed at the time. Mama would be home any minute. When she got inside her house, she shoved the drawing tablet under her bed, grabbed her sneakers from out front, undressed, threw the clothes and sneakers in the washer, and jumped in the shower. When she was done, she turned on the washer and toothbrushed the grout in both bathrooms. She was fast. She'd just stepped out of the utility room and tossed the clothes into the dryer when Mama came home.

"Oh, you *are* my best girl," Mama said, noting the whirring of the dryer. But, as she always did, Mama checked.

"Nealy, what is this you're drying?"

"My clothes," Nealy said, though she knew the reason for the question.

"Why didn't you wait until you had a full load?" Yes, this was rule number one when doing laundry at the Comptons'.

"I, uh, they were really dirty."

"Have you been over at that house?" First a question, then a statement. "You've been over there and gotten black. I thought I told you to stay away from there."

"You did, Mama, but ..." She was caught between truth and lie.

"Don't you *but* me, young lady." Mama grabbed a handful of hair and jounced Nealy up, then set her down. "What have you been doing over there, where you have no business?"

Grabbing the top of her head, but refraining from howling, Nealy lied about what she'd been doing. "I've been helping." She surprised herself with this evasion.

"Helping! Helping with what?"

"Well"—and she harked back to something one of the fire fighters had said last night at the fire—"if we get that wet debris out of the house, there's a chance most of the floors will be okay."

Mama examined her for several minutes, searching between truth and lie herself. But Nealy was her best girl. Mama had said it herself. "All right, then, if you're really helping. Heaven knows you don't mind getting filthy."

"I was black," Nealy said. "Only the whites of my eyeballs showed."

Mama laughed a little, as much as she ever laughed. She walked through the house, checking in every room, including both bathrooms and the utility room. Nodding her okay, she opened the refrigerator and pulled out some things for supper.

"We have these leftover chicken fajitas, which we can have with a fruit salad," Mama said, more to herself than to Nealy. Nealy knew her job and didn't mind doing it. She set the table the way Mama liked, with the placemats and the sterling silver. They used to use it only on rare occasions but one day Mama had said, "What am I saving this for?" and they had started using it every day.

Nealy used the cloth napkins, and put plates, salt, and pepper on the table and ice and tea in the royal blue glasses.

At the table, they ate in silence. Sometimes Nealy chattered, but Mama never did. Tonight the things running through Nealy's mind were either private, personal things or things that would upset Mama, so she was quiet. Mama didn't notice.

After dinner, they cleared away the dishes and cleaned the kitchen. Mama removed the burner rings and cleaned under them. So Noel Anne thought Nealy was a slavey. But Mama did these things, too. She didn't go sit down and leave it all to Nealy. Nealy thought it was fair to do her share. In fact, she thought it was so stupid, all those kids whose mothers did everything for them. She liked feeling competent. She just wished, well ... she stopped the wish. It seemed she'd been wishing it all day, all week, all year. Maybe all her life.

Hands doubly, triply clean now, she picked up her drawing tablet. "I'm going down the street to try to remember the tree and draw it, okay?" The *okay* was just for politeness. As long as she did her chores, behaved herself, and was home by dark, Mama usually didn't much mind where she went or how long she stayed.

"Are you still worrying about that tree?"

Nealy propped the edge of the tablet on her hip. "No, not worrying. I just wish they hadn't taken it down. And I wish I'd drawn it before, because already I can't remember it exactly." Mama was involved with the crossword puzzle in *TV Guide,* and Nealy left.

Even from the corner of Amherst, three blocks away from where the tree had been, Dartmouth Street looked empty. There was no sign of the huge old oak, not even a stump. They must have wrenched the roots out of the earth. She'd seen them do it before, with a tree that really was already dead. It was like pulling a molar of the giant Orion. They had used grappling hooks and cables, but the roots ran deep and stretched out as broadly as the limbs had stretched above it. This live tree must have fought ferociously. She hadn't known they could even do all that in one day.

As she came closer she saw a stake sticking up where the tree had been. Someone had planted a live-oak sapling. It would be a hundred years before this slender one was the size of the other.

But here was a special tree she could watch grow. They grew for a hundred years, lived strong and healthy for another hundred, and took a hundred to decline. Experts on live oaks had learned this by studying the notes and notebooks of early settlers who had mentioned particular trees.

First she sketched the sapling as it was, then she projected it through the years until it was enormous, making it look as much as she could like the one it had replaced. She would tell her children and her grandchildren the story of this tree, and when her grandchildren were old, they would tell their grandchildren.

She was as pleased with her drawings as she was surprised at her thoughts. She didn't even believe in growing up, and here she was thinking about her grandchildren's grandchildren!

When she got home, reality pounced. Daddy was there, and he and Mama were arguing about Noel Anne.

7
Accused

On Saturday morning, her lie about helping came true. When she looked out to see how the day was starting, cars were pulling up in front of Mrs. Dees's house. Before Nealy thought, she sprinted right over. From the porch, Mrs. Dees skewered her.

"Didn't I ask you to please stay away?"

Stunned, Nealy stopped. Without turning, she retreated, feeling it unsafe to turn her back. A man stared, and she felt skewered twice.

As she backed across the street a truck rumbled along and she jumped out of the way. The truck was towing a long, green, open-topped trailer. Both truck and trailer were stamped with black letters: CITY OF HANOVER. Yeah, she thought. The same suckers who took down the oak tree. The truck backed the trailer into the yard, up to the edge of Mrs. Dees's porch. The man who'd stared at her motioned to her to come over, strange hand signals that seemed to mean for her to come hide behind the trailer. Finally she darted back over.

"Here. You can watch from behind the sway cart," he said, patting the trailer. "After a while, I'll have something for you to do." So, lurking behind the green trailer, she was able to watch. People with gloved hands carried black debris out of the house, either piece by piece or in garbage cans.

"One five-inch owl," someone called out, setting a small blackened owl on the edge of the porch.

"Eight each dinner plates, salad plates, and bowls," said someone else.

"One meltdown of vacuum cleaner."

Mrs. Dees, carrying a luminous royal blue acrylic clipboard, walked back and forth, in and out of the house, and Nealy realized she was making a list of everything people called out to her.

The meltdown of vacuum cleaner made a tremendous crash when it was tossed into the trailer they called a sway cart. The blackened dishes were set at the edge of the porch with the owl. Other people named items and threw them into the sway cart. Garbage cans full of debris were also upended.

"Why are you putting those things on the porch?" Mrs. Dees asked.

"We think they'll clean up," said the man who had secreted Nealy behind the sway cart.

"No!" Mrs. Dees's screams startled several other people as well as Nealy. "No! No! I don't want charred souvenirs of fire." As she shrieked Mrs. Dees grabbed several of the items and pitched them wildly. The blackened owl landed on the ground with an unbroken thud. "Throw them away; throw them away." Crying and yelling as wildly as she threw, she smashed another object on the sidewalk.

"I don't want *any* . . ."

. . . she pitched . . .

". . . of it." She pitched again.

One item caromed off the side of the sway cart, and the last clipped the edge and bounced in.

"Hey, you're getting better," someone hollered. A cheer went up, and someone moved to take Mrs. Dees's hand and hug her.

In a cracked voice, Mrs. Dees said, "I don't want any of it."

"Okay, okay," said Nealy's protector to Mrs. Dees. He scooped up the stack of dishes and headed for the sway cart. Before Nealy knew what he was doing, he was holding out the dishes to her. "Quick," he said. "Take them and set them carefully behind the tree. Then come back and start pitching things into the sway cart."

Nealy nestled the dishes out of sight between some tree roots. When she returned, the man had hoisted one of the debris-laden garbage cans down off the porch. "Pitch," he said, winking. "As long as she hears the crash of things being thrown in, she'll be okay."

As she pitched pieces of she-didn't-know-what, he took more things around behind the tree.

"Ten books," someone called out.

Mrs. Dees wrote.

"One end table."

Mrs. Dees wrote.

"Part of a picture frame, about two feet by three feet. Do you know what it was?"

"Oh." Mrs. Dees put her hand to her mouth. "That must have been my Charlotte Harrell painting." She lowered her hand and wrote.

"What are they doing?" Nealy asked.

"Making a record for the insurance company," the man told her.

"Ooooohhhh," Nealy said, thinking how awful it must be to have to examine everything and try to figure out what it once was.

"Keep throwing," the man said, handing down another loaded garbage can and returning the empty one to the porch. Happy to be helping, Nealy saw that they were distracting Mrs. Dees. The woman didn't notice the things being whisked away and hidden behind the tree. Nealy thought she agreed with Mrs. Dees. Why would anyone want to keep those thoroughly charred things? Nealy pitched and pitched.

Another pitcher started singing "Yo ho heave ho" until everyone was singing. Those pitching heaved on the word *heave.* Those coming in and out of the house with things and debris set things down on the *heave.*

"How do you tell your friends you've been through a devastating house fire?" someone asked.

"Should we design a line of greeting cards?" said Mrs. Dees's daughter, Adriana.

"I regret to inform you . . ." a man said.

". . . that my house burned," someone else finished.

Everyone was as black as Nealy had been, and probably was again. The most prominent feature on every face was the whites of the eyes. Someone *kerchew*ed a vociferous sneeze.

"Who's got some tissues?"

"They burned."

Neighbors from the other corner came over with two trays, one with two pitchers of iced tea and the other with plenty of glasses. And napkins.

"Napkins!" said the one who'd asked for tissues. He took one and blew his nose. "I even have black boogers."

"Soot!" someone said, as a curse word.

"We'll get your beautiful glasses filthy," Mrs. Dees said as the trays were set on the end of the porch.

"Don't worry. They'll wash."

"What the soot, then." Glasses were lifted and clinked together.

"Cheers."

"L'chaim."

"Toujours gai."

Nealy stood on the fringes enjoying it all. Even Mrs. Dees was laughing.

But in the calm of resting and drinking tea, Mrs. Dees glanced around and saw Nealy.

"What are you doing here?" The joy left the air. "I thought I asked you to stay away."

Everyone was stiff and silent. Panic was in Mrs. Dees's voice and panic weakened Nealy's legs as she backed away.

The man who'd kept her throwing bobbed his head and nodded toward the tree. Yes, the tree. It was the nearest place to get out of sight. She ducked behind it. Following, the man lifted some of the hidden dishes and smuggled them into his orange truck, which was parked behind the tree.

"These will clean up," he said. "Can you come with me? Are you a good scrubber?"

Nervousness and truth made her giggle. She *was* a good scrubber.

"You live right there?" He pointed across at her house. "Ask your mother if you can come with me. Never mind." He started across the street. "I'll ask." He beat Nealy to the door, glanced at his sooty knuckles, and knocked with his elbow.

Mama came to the door and drew back in surprise at the two of them. "Nealy?"

"Yes, ma'am."

"Hobby? Frankie Habich?" Mama said to the man.

"Yes, ma'am. I'm taking some ceramic stuff over to my house to see if I can clean it up and I wondered if Nealy could come help me."

"You still live over on Duchess Street?" Mama moved her head toward her left shoulder.

"Yeah. I live upstairs and rent downstairs, and my last tenant moved out just in time for Mrs. Dees to move in."

"What a good thing for her."

"Yes. I told her I can't believe all the miracles she's having in the midst of disaster."

"What else?" Mama asked.

"The only part of her house not destroyed was her ceramic studio in the back room."

"Is that right?"

"Ceramic studio?" Nealy didn't even know Mrs. Dees had a ceramic studio.

But Mama was answering Frankie Habich about Nealy coming with him. "If she wants to, sure."

As the two of them crossed back to the car, he

held up a charcoal finger and said, "Just a minute."

When he came back, he had the smoke-blackened whale door knocker from Mrs. Dees's front door. "I think we can clean this, too."

"The door doesn't even look damaged," she said. "Isn't that weird?"

Mr. Habich laughed. "You should see the back of it. The inside side. Totally charred. What's left is about a quarter-inch thick."

"Really?"

"Really, Nealy. So, your name is Nealy. Mine's Hobby."

Yes, she knew that the same way he knew hers. Mama had said both names. She both wanted and didn't want to know where Mama knew this man from. Mama knew lots of men. She was afraid to ask.

He drove down Dartmouth Street, by where the tree had been, and she cried out.

The sapling was gone and the street was paved over.

Hobby pulled over. "Yup. Now those stupidheads have taken out the sapling. Suddenly, after two hundred years, it's dangerous to have a tree in the middle of the street, even though the street clearly goes around it."

Nealy nodded.

"Did you hear that? That people had crashed into it? I say anyone who can't see an enormous tree in the middle of the road ought not to be driving."

"Really." She sagged against the door and stared at the curving curb. Strange memorial for a tree, a bend in curbstone and a wide swath of asphalt.

"They're going to take others out, too. The ones in the streets and the ones that bulge into the street. They're going to straighten the streets."

"What?" She looked at Hobby, not believing that what she'd popped out with to Bobby and the others was true. "You mean the one in the middle of Prince, near King? You mean the one that bulges off the curb on Amherst Street?" She knew them and named them all. "Can't we do anything about it?"

"There was a meeting. Five hundred people came to protest. But . . ." He gestured toward the treeless space. "You see."

"I wish I had some green paint," she said. "I'd paint a huge tree in the middle of the street."

"That's the best idea I've heard lately," he said as he drove on to the hardware store, where he bought steel wool, a steel scrub brush, cleanser, and brass polish.

"Will these things really clean up?"

"You watch and see. They're glass and ceramic. When they were made, they were fired at a much hotter heat than this fire."

At the house, he opened the door. Inside, the house was empty. No furniture. No bed. Apparently Mrs. Dees wasn't staying here yet. In the kitchen there was a double sink, and they set to scrubbing side by side.

"Baked-on black," Hobby said, taking a black glass and handing her another. "What color do you think is underneath?"

"I don't know." She watched to see how he began.

"Let's see who can find out the fastest," he said, charging the glass with cleanser and an abrasive scrubber. She did the same.

"Blue!" she said, surprised to see a spot of bright blue.

"Yeah." He showed her that he'd scrubbed through to blue, too.

It was surprising how easily the objects cleaned up. She'd thought the black was baked on forever.

The glass was a bright, clear blue, the color of the clipboard Mrs. Dees had been carrying.

The only hard thing about the scrubbing was that there was so much of it. Two things broke from cracks, but almost everything else cleaned up. The dishes—dinner plates, salad plates, and bowls—were white with a blue spiral from center to rim.

"She made these," he said.

"Mrs. Dees made her own dishes?"

"And this," he said, showing her the once-blackened owl, now blue. A smooth, stylized owl. Nealy saw herself making squirrels and insects and butterflies. And her own dishes.

"I think she likes blue, don't you?" Hobby said.

"Her bike is blue, too," Nealy said. "Or it was."

"Oh, yeah. Whoever took it has probably painted it green by now."

"Yeah," she said. She knew from Daddy how fast bicycles and cars could be disguised by re-painting.

"I've known your mom and dad for a long time," Hobby said as he set sparkling dishes into the previously empty cabinets.

"Really?" Since he'd mentioned Daddy, too, it seemed safer to comment.

"Really, Nealy. We were in high school to-gether right here in Hanover."

"You were?" Somehow Hobby seemed younger than her parents.

"Oh, yeah. They were the great lovers of high school."

"They were?" She was astonished, but glad to hear it, glad to know that someone knew they had loved each other once. Ever since she'd known them, they'd been great haters. She thought of them arguing about Noel Anne last night. Mama wanted Daddy to take Noel Anne home to live with them. Daddy wouldn't, of course. It was a pointless request. Daddy liked to come around and act like he cared, but he didn't. Not only was he not there every day, he was not there on any regular basis you could count on. Not once a week, or once every two weeks, or even once a month. Whenever it suited him, he came around. He never thought about what might suit anyone else.

She dried the last glass and held it to the light.

"Mama likes blue, too."

Hobby took it and added it to the shelves of glistening dishes and they both said, "Beautiful."

"And they said it couldn't be done," he said.

"I would have said it couldn't be done."

Now he scrubbed and polished the door knocker with brass polish and when it was gleaming, he motioned her to follow. At the front door, she watched with satisfaction as he fastened the bright brass whale.

8

A Chance to Help

All weekend, people helped in all kinds of ways. Twice on Saturday and twice on Sunday the sway cart was filled.

In addition to saving the floors by getting the wet debris out of the house, as the fire fighters had said, someone said it would also help with the smoke smell.

"I think it's embedded in my nostrils forever," the next-door neighbor, Ms. Royster, said. "And those flames are always at the edge of my eyeballs."

Nealy nodded. Even when she was away from the neighborhood, she smelled smoke. And at unexpected moments, there was fire in her face.

Especially in her dreams. She saw Daddy in flames, and Noel Anne. Huge trees in flames waving fiery arms, unable to run from the fire. Being unable to run was a dream she had sometimes. Waking in the night, she concentrated on the least fearful thing: the tree. Perhaps she really could paint one in the street. She lay awake thinking about how to do it quickly and efficiently.

Though she knew she should stay away, she kept hanging around Mrs. Dees's house. Her house. She was compelled to be there. Hobby gave her ways to help that would keep her out of Mrs. Dees's sight.

A dresser was brought out from Mrs. Dees's studio and it was okay except for soot. Two women started cleaning it and Nealy, because of the soot inside the jewelry box, suggested they clean inside the drawers, too.

"It's only on the outside," one of the women said, wiping and wiping. "It couldn't get inside the drawers. Look how tightly they overlap."

When she couldn't get them to listen, Nealy just moved up to the dresser and opened a drawer.

Soot.

"Look at this!" the other woman exclaimed.

"Would you have believed this?" Everyone came over to see.

"How did you know?" the first woman asked.

"Well . . ." Nealy certainly wasn't going to say she kept a stolen jewelry box under Mrs. Dees's house and it had soot inside. She shrugged. "I've had experience with soot."

The same neighbors walked over with iced tea and another brought a pot of coffee and someone else came with a tray of sandwiches. Nealy was impressed with the generosity, but she knew she wasn't welcome for this feast, so she ran home and made her own.

When she returned, people were bringing all kinds of other things for Mrs. Dees. A toaster oven. A bed with mattress and box spring, pillows, and even sheets and pillowcases. Towels. A chair.

"Put them in my truck," Hobby requested as they looked for a clean place to put the things down. "I'll take them over for her later."

Nealy hung out by the truck while the mattress was loaded, and then he noticed her.

He winked. "You okay?"

She nodded, but he must have known her feelings.

"Hey, come here." He beckoned with a finger,

then put it to his mouth for secrecy, and she followed him to the house. Such work going on! The main debris was out, but they were literally shoveling soot. They were ripping out the burned walls.

"It was a quick flash fire," Hobby told her. "It destroyed almost everything visible—furniture, pictures, light fixtures, the wall—but it didn't burn into the studs behind the wall." He showed her the light wood of the framing behind the blackened wall. "That's how they know it was arson. Nothing else would have burned it so fast."

Arson. She cringed. How could being in the house make her feel guilty, as though she really had been the one to do it? Did Hobby know Mrs. Dees thought it was she? Or did he think Mrs. Dees didn't want her around because she was a pest? A horrendous roar provided distraction, and Hobby apparently thought she was cringing be-cause of the noise.

"Vacuuming," he said. "In order to get the smoke smell out, we have to clean the soot off the floor, too. Out of the cracks between the floorboards."

He didn't have to tell her. She had her own proof of soot sifting between the floorboards.

"Look," he said, but she was already staring.

In the hall, right in a doorway, there were two huge wood-brown footprints surrounded by charred floor. She gasped. It couldn't be true, but it looked like someone had stood right there in the midst of the fire.

Hobby grinned. "Doesn't it give you the shivers?"

"Yessssss." She remembered the fire fighter's denial.

Then Hobby told her about the footprints. Mrs. Dees had told him that this doorway had been walled off years ago, and she had put a long, built-in desk in the hall in front of the spot where the doorway had been. One of her grown and gone sons had long ago left a pair of shoes under the desk, and the shoes had never been moved. During the fire, the desk and shoes had burned, and the wall had burned away from the old door frame. But the shoes had kept the floor beneath them from burning, and these eerie footprints were left.

Hobby shivered himself and led her to the back.

"The miracle room," he said. Mrs. Dees's studio. The ceiling and upper walls were just as charred as everything else, but a char line angled across the wall from three to four feet above the floor. Below that line everything was covered with soot but otherwise okay. The color of the wall was even visible.

"How come it didn't burn down here?"

He pointed out a narrow fringe of white near the bottom of the charred wall in the back hall. Moving from there through the next room and into the studio, the white fringe broadened in a steady, straight line. It was as though someone had measured it off and drawn it with a ruler.

"Measured by fire," she said.

"By heat rising," he said. "You've learned about fire safety, haven't you? How you're supposed to get down on the floor and crawl?"

Nealy nodded. "Yes."

"This is why. Even if there's an inferno, you may be safe crawling out under it. You wouldn't have survived up front, obviously, but back here it wasn't deadly hot near the floor. Look."

On one of the tables, bundles of clay lay wrapped in plastic, and the plastic hadn't even melted.

"Isn't it a miracle that everything in her house was destroyed except the most important thing, her work?"

"Yes," Nealy said again. But she was more interested to see that Mrs. Dees had this whole life she knew nothing about. Adriana had never mentioned that her mother had a studio. Or if she had, Nealy guessed she had been too young to be interested or even know what that meant.

On the floor stood a potter's wheel and a kiln. Stacked shelves climbed the walls and were filled with various types of pottery and clay sculpture. Weird pots and bowls and other shapes. Figures of people. Animals formed with abstract, stylized lines. Black, they were all black from the fire. Black or not, the studio looked like a place where magic was made. Nealy wanted her hands in clay.

"How good are you at going out windows?" Hobby said abruptly. When she looked at him, he indicated something with a motion of his head. She got it. Mrs. Dees was coming that way.

"Meet me at the truck," he said in a loud whisper as she stepped onto the back windowsill and soared out over a hedge of ligustrum.

In a few minutes he came to the truck, and she rode with him to take the load of things over to his house, to Mrs. Dees's new place.

"Was she surprised to see her stuff all clean?"

"She was so amazed she cried."

As they carried the things into the house he repeated his list of miracles. Nobody being hurt. The studio not being destroyed. His having his downstairs apartment vacant. All the people gathering around to help.

Nealy nodded. She guessed those were miracles of a sort, except that when she thought of miracles, she thought more in terms of the house being miraculously restored overnight, or of the Dartmouth Street oak tree growing gloriously again.

As if reading her thoughts, he said, "Have you thought any more about painting a tree in the street?"

She looked at him for a moment, trying to figure out what he was thinking. Adults were so unpredictable.

"You have, haven't you?" His grin gave her confidence.

"Well, yeah. I've figured out how to do it quickly."

"Oh, yeah? How's that?"

"Just draw a big, puffy shape for the main part of the tree and two lines for the trunk." With her forefinger, she drew it in the air.

He took hold of her elbow and squeezed it.

"Let's go get some paint." In a jiffy they were at Princess and River streets, at Hanover Hardware. She'd been in here on errands for Mama. Picture hooks or, yes, rug cleaner. She laughed at that. Almost everything Mama needed but groceries, Nealy ran the errand for it. Mama was not a shopper.

Hobby moved through the store, leading her to a rack with bookmark-sized cards with zillions of colors on them.

"What are these for?" she asked.

"Paint chips, so we can pick a color."

"Green," she said, and he handed her swatches of green.

"How about one of these?" He pointed to a dark green called Evening Shadows, which was about the color of live-oak leaves.

She squinted, as though seeing it on the street. "Won't it be too dark to show up enough on the black street?"

"Smart girl. I think you're right. You pick one."

The names of the colors enchanted her. Gumdrop, Garden Fantasy, Green Melody, Merry Green, Green Thumb, Everglade. Somebody must have had fun thinking of all those names.

"Everglade," she said. Everglade was a bright

medium green and should show up well on the street.

The salesclerk was beside them. "How much? And what is it you're going to paint?"

Hobby winked at her and said, "Lawn furniture. Two lawn chairs. I think a quart will be enough."

Then, to her surprise, the clerk pried the top off the can. The paint was white.

"Green," she said. "Everglade."

The clerk and Hobby both laughed. "This is just base white," the clerk said. "We mix it to order."

There were stacks and stacks and stacks of paint cans. "You mean all this is white?"

"Yes," he said. "Except that if you wanted white, we'd mix in some yellow or blue or gray or orange, depending on the exact tone of white you wanted." He looked at a code of numbers for Everglade and began to squirt colors into the white paint. He squirted a lot of yellow and dark green and, to her surprise, four squirts of brown.

"Brown?" Was he messing up their order?

"Umber," he said as he tapped the lid back on and strapped the can into a machine that shimmied and shook.

"And how about a brush?" he asked while the paint wobbled.

"I have plenty of brushes," Hobby said.

When the machine stopped shaking, the clerk removed the top of the white-yellow-green-brown paint and there was Everglade, the color of the future tree. She and Hobby nodded to each other in pleasure.

"That was fun," she said. "I never knew buying paint was so complicated."

Hobby laughed at her delight. "You're easy to please," he said as they walked back to the truck.

"See you at nine-thirty, then," Hobby said as he parked in front of Nealy's house. This painting deed required darkness, and for now he was going back over to work at Mrs. Dees's. "In fact, why don't I come in right now and ask your mom if you can help me with something tonight?"

Nealy wondered what he was going to tell Mama he needed help with at that hour. It turned out not to be a problem. Mama wasn't home. But Noel Anne was.

9

The Painted Tree

"Noel Anne!" Nealy shrieked, so happy to see her home. She made quick introductions between Noel Anne and Hobby, who stood at the door.

"I'll talk to your mom later," he said, and he left.

"Mama's new boyfriend?" Noel Anne's voice held more than a thimbleful of scorn.

"No. He knows Mama. Daddy, too. But he's *my* friend."

The subject of boyfriends was pointless to her. Noel Anne and Mama both had plenty and they each thought the other should not. Mama thought Noel Anne was too young and Noel Anne thought Mama was too old.

"Where did Mama go?" Nealy asked, nervous about getting out of the house that night.

Noel Anne shrugged. "She wasn't here when I got here."

For a moment Nealy felt trouble coming. Had she left the door unlocked? Mama would be furious, regardless of how Noel Anne had come in, because she'd told number-one daughter not to come back. And being a police officer's family had made them especially conscious of security. But no, it wasn't her fault. When she and Hobby had left to move things, Mama had been here. Thoughts rolled and clicked in Nealy's head, because Mama never left the door unlocked.

"How did you get in, then?"

"This is my home." Noel Anne stretched her arms and hands as though in welcome to herself.

"But . . ."

"But, but, but. I know, Mama changed the lock. What she said when I left was, if you go out that door, not to ever come back through it. And I didn't. I didn't come in by the door."

Great _uh-ohs_ rolled through Nealy. She saw Noel Anne again, three days ago, pulling that door open in spite of what Mama said, and smiling pertly as she walked on out.

"What have you been doing?" Nealy asked, to avoid the issue of how Noel Anne had gotten in. "Where are you staying, then?"

"None of your beeswax." Noel Anne grinned. Always so saucy, so sure, Nealy thought.

"Does Mama know where you're staying?"

"It's none of her beeswax, either. It's good being away from her."

Nealy clamped her fist to her lips. Did Noel Anne really think she was out from under Mama's authority? Lowering her hand, she said, "Mama's not so bad."

"Oh, yeah? How many times has she smacked you since I left?"

Nealy felt again the sting of Mama's hand across her face the morning after the fire, even before she had been awake enough to know what was happening. "Once," she said, and was immediately sorry she had answered the question. "But she had reason. I had been over at the fire. . . ."

"Yeah, I saw. What in the world happened?"

Nealy told her about it, glad for the distraction.

"So that's when Mama slapped you? When she saw you had crawled in bed all sooty?"

"I just didn't think," Nealy said. "You know how Mama is."

"Yes. A clean-a-holic."

Nealy shrugged. "I just try to do what Mama says and try to do things even before she asks."

"You're such a goody-goody."

"I just like my money." Nealy squirmed and tucked her feet up under her. "Anyway, I'm glad you're home." They were quiet for a minute, fast-mouthed Noel Anne not having any more response to feelings than Mama did.

"Noel Anne, I'm the one who took the jewelry box."

"Well, I know that."

"How did you know?"

"Well, I knew I didn't take it, and who else is there?"

Nealy blushed. "I'm sorry."

"Okay, well, you be sorry about it and you do what you have to do about it, but you know that doesn't really have anything to do with the trouble between me and Mama."

Nealy turned that over and over in her head. She knew the missing jewelry box wasn't the trouble between Noel Anne and Mama, but she'd thought Noel Anne would turn it into the biggest thing.

"How *did* you get in?" she asked, finally.

"My bedroom window. I broke it."

"Noel Anne! You broke it? Why in the world? Why didn't you just go to Mama's office and ask to come home?"

"Ha!"

Nealy didn't understand why people did what they did, acted the way they acted. Herself included. Herself, the thief. Even if the jewelry box was only a tiny part of the things that had set Mama off. Even if she had truly tried to say she'd taken it, which had only angered Mama more. Even if Mama wanted to think everything was Noel Anne's fault. Nealy was the one who was responsible for the jewelry box.

When they heard Mama's car in the driveway, Noel Anne stood up and waited boldly.

"I didn't come in the door," Noel Anne announced as Mama came through it.

After the merest glance at Noel Anne, Mama looked at Nealy.

"I just came in and here she was," Nealy said.

When Mama walked down the hall, Nealy wanted to leap out the door and dive under Mrs. Dees's house. Instead, she looked over Noel Anne's shoulder at a watercolor Mama had painted when she was in college in Tallahassee.

It was a streetscape, and Nealy searched it, eye-walking the street, looking for a safe place.

Back in the living room, Mama picked up the phone, dialed.

"I've had a break-in," she said, giving her name and address. "Can you send a car around?"

Noel Anne stomped a foot and rolled her eyes. "Mama, you're kidding, right? You act so crazy."

Nealy disappeared into the picture.

Mama stood drumming her fingers on the phone. Nealy decided that Mama had just faked the call—until a police car pulled up in front of the house.

The policeman who came was Daddy. His partner, Brian, stayed in the car.

"This girl broke into my house," Mama said, indicating Noel Anne.

"Oh, Marilyn, for pity's sake," Daddy said. "What's wrong now?"

Daddy looked disgusted, as though he wished he were anywhere but here. Didn't he know that she was here, too? Couldn't he wink or say, "Hi, Nealy"?

"I just told you," Mama said. "This girl smashed a window and broke in."

"This girl is your daughter."

"Yours, too."

Daddy stalked through the house and Nealy followed. Sure enough, the window in Noel Anne's room was broken. Glass was scattered across the bedspread.

"See? Do you see? I want her charged with breaking and entering."

"Marilyn, what the ..."

As Daddy's voice trailed off Nealy reached for the trash can and began picking glass off the bed.

"Mary Neal, leave it," Mama said from the doorway. "That's evidence. I am not kidding, David. She is not supposed to be in this house. I want her out of here and I want her charged."

"Marilyn, she's fourteen years old. She's your daughter."

They were back in the living room and they could all complete the chorus of "She's yours, too," though Mama didn't say it this time.

"Well, you figure out what to do with her, then. That's your job."

Nealy's breath stuck somewhere in her throat. She looked around for her safe place in the Tallahassee picture but there was no safe place. The afternoon light sparkled off every glass object in the room. The prism cast rainbows, as though everything were right with the world.

She made herself deaf, dumb, and blind and missed the next exchanges until Dad, the policeman, was yanking a reluctant Noel Anne out the door.

"At least let me get some clothes," Noel Anne said, leaning away from Daddy and back into the house, but he gripped her wrist and kept moving.

"I've worn these same clothes for days!" Noel Anne protested. Nealy kept her mouth shut. She'd taken Noel Anne two changes of clothes. Dad disappeared, then Noel Anne, with her free arm swinging up behind her, reaching back. Mama closed the door behind them.

"I'm glad to know you didn't let her in," her mother said, breaking their silence. Turning toward Nealy, Mama leaned for a moment as if for a hug, but she stopped and sat on the sofa, silent.

Nealy thought she would hold her breath forever.

Finally, Mama said, "Thank you, Mary Neal. I don't know what I'd do without you. You are my best girl."

Mama, I'm not your best girl, she thought. All

she could see in her mind's eye was Noel Anne's hand reaching back. She wanted to tell Mama about the jewelry box, but she wanted to return it clean and restored. Besides, telling right now would not heal anything. It would deprive Mama of her best girl. Mama needed something, too, didn't she? When Hobby came, Nealy wouldn't go. She'd stay here with Mama. What neither she nor Mama needed right now was to have Nealy caught defacing public property.

In the meantime, she chewed the inside of her lips and hypnotized herself with one of her nature videos. Young bear cubs emerged from their den for the first time and caterwauled at the strangeness. The mother heard. The mother came. Isn't that what mothers did? Be comforting and take care of the young? She thought of the marsh hen gathering the chicks. Mama always seemed to be pushing away. All Nealy wanted was to have Mama gather her in.

When Hobby came and before Nealy could say no, she wasn't going, Mama pushed away again, waving her arm and saying, "Go, go."

Nealy went.

"What was that all about?" Hobby asked.

Nealy had no idea what to say, so she mimicked

Mama's arm waving. "Oh, you know parents." As he drove away she asked, "Do you have kids?"

"No. I'm not married. But I remember parents."

Instead of driving to the "tree" place, he drove past it and around the corner to his house. Mrs. Dees's car was there, too.

"See what I've got?" he said. He showed her some things from a paper bag. The paint. An old paintbrush. Several narrow, slender paddles to stir the paint with. A screwdriver.

"What's that for?"

He made motions with the screwdriver. "To pry off the lid of the paint can."

"Oh," she said. She hadn't thought of that. If she had been doing this by herself, she would have gotten down there and not been able to open the can.

"And . . ." He lifted a whisk broom out of the sack. "For?" he asked.

She knew immediately what it was for because she had thought of that one herself. "To clean the street."

He smiled his approval. "We'll leave the car here and walk over. That way there won't be an incriminating car on the street."

They walked inside dark shadows and through

pools of light from the streetlights. Nealy wanted to skulk along in the shadows and dash through the puddles of light, but they merely strolled. On Dartmouth Street, Hobby sat down where the curb curved, next to some azalea bushes.

"Here, you whisk the street while I open the can," he said.

Before she moved, she checked the street forty-two times, then stepped out, whisking the area and darting back to cover.

Hobby had the lid off and held out the brush and can to her.

"Me?" she squeaked.

"It was your idea. I'll be your lookout. If I see a car coming, I'll let you know and you can scamper over here by the azaleas, to the side away from the headlights. How long do you think it will take?"

She'd thought about it when she figured out how to draw the tree as a cloud shape with lines for the trunk. "One minute." Hobby stepped toward the corner and she moved back into the street. With a dip and a stroke, she began. Dip, stroke, dip, stroke, dip, stroke. She painted the three-foot-by-four-foot bulk of the tree. Her heart drummed in her chest and her throat. Dip, stroke for one side of the trunk—and she heard a car. She grabbed the can and ran so fast she almost sloshed the paint. Before she reached cover, the car had whizzed by on the cross street. Hobby was laughing.

"I'm watching. I saw it wasn't going to turn."

"But what if they saw me? What if they come back to look?"

"They're not turning around. Go ahead and finish."

She returned to complete the job. After she made the second side of the trunk, she was inspired to paint the word *tree* under it. Then she returned to the first side and added the word *tree.*

Back in the cover of the azaleas, Hobby used the handle of the screwdriver to tamp the lid back on the can. The tapping sounded louder than the music box had under Mrs. Dees's house.

"Stand for examination," Hobby said when they were at his truck. She stood, arms out, turning slowly while they both searched for any telltale signs of Everglade. Not finding any, he congratulated her and took her home. They'd been gone for twenty minutes. She expected Mama to question, to say, "That was quick, what in the world was it?" But Mama was already in bed.

Undressed and in bed, Nealy was staring, even with her eyes closed. Images, like the too-quick changing of television channels, flickered behind her eyelids. Paint, painting, fire, tree, Hobby, headlights, Mama, Noel Anne, soot, paint, Daddy, headlights, green, green, Everglade green.

10
Found Out

In the morning, Nealy sat on the curb staring into the space of the painted tree. It was gorgeous. She was glad they'd done it, but it wasn't a real tree a hundred feet high and a hundred feet wide and three hundred years old. If five hundred people at the meeting couldn't do anything about the trees, then she couldn't, either. At least most of the cars that drove by curved with the curb, as if the tree were still there. They didn't run over the painted tree.

Strolling by Hobby's house, she gazed at the lower story, where Mrs. Dees now lived. This house, too, was built several feet above the ground, not like Nealy's house, which was built on a concrete slab on the ground. It surprised her to realize that she was wondering if there was comfortable space underneath. Why did she want to hang around Mrs. Dees? Did she remind her of Grandma? Someone who did okay with life? Was it, now that she knew about it, because Mrs. Dees made magic with clay the way Nealy made magic with drawing pencils?

There was this guy, Christo, who made huge and crazy art, like setting enormous umbrellas across eighteen miles of California hills and valleys. Some people had argued about that, saying it was stupid and it wasn't art, while others had come from all over to see it, even from other countries. When she'd seen it on television, those yellow umbrellas looked like bright flowers that had floated down to dot the landscape and delight the world.

As she walked down King Street she chirped, barked, meowed, and clucked at every critter she saw, then irritated Noel Anne by going into the Yogurt Shoppe. In the Queen Street Book Shop, she asked Mrs. Frazier if she could put the butterfly book away for her, and Mrs. Frazier reached under the counter and showed her she already had the book set aside with Nealy's name on it.

To celebrate, she crossed to Grand Square and walked round and round the circular sidewalk. After the third circumnavigation she began to run, and the next time around she almost collided with a flock of lawyers coming out of a building. Embarrassed, she crossed to Princess and moseyed by the school and beyond, past Sidney Lanier Boulevard, until she was on the bridge above the tidal canal. She neither saw nor heard the marsh chicks. They'd probably grown into their camouflage by now. They'd probably learned quickly how to stay hidden.

By Wednesday, people had stopped coming to Mrs. Dees's house, even Mrs. Dees. Most everyone had helped all they could, Nealy guessed, and had to go back to work or something. When no one had come by ten, she crossed the street and made the double duck under the yellow tape and through the lattice to reclaim her territory.

When she lifted the shirt from the top of the box, she sighed and shook her head. After all her recent experience with soot, why had she thought a piece of cloth would keep out soot?

"Soot!" she said, using it as a swear word, as the workers had. "Soot, soot, soot!" It was a most satisfying word. Taking the shirt a few feet away, she shook it out, then blew soot off the bugs, the books, the jewelry box. Balancing everything in her lap, she turned the empty cardboard box over and tapped out the soot. All the traipsing back and forth in the house above had rained soot below. Of course.

Leaning against the brick column, she started thinking about how to draw the fire. Could she make the flames lick out the windows? Could she sketch the dark-eyed house after the fire, as it was now? She thought of drawing the oak tree and got an idea to make a guide to the live oaks of Hanover. Maybe that's what she'd do for her work, make magic with field guides. Already she had thought about a field guide to dogs. The only dog books she knew about gave either too little information or too much. She wanted to make a small, compact field guide to dogs. Probably she could puts cats in the same volume.

As she laughed at herself for having too many ambitions, she heard the slam of a car door, followed by multiple voices and footsteps. Someone was coming to work after all. As whoever it was walked above her she could tell exactly which areas had been vacuumed and which had not. Certain footsteps caused a shower of soot and others, like those above her in the hallway, did not. Just above her the steps stopped. No doubt they were exclaiming again over the eerie foot-prints.

Suddenly there was a sawing sound above her. She jumped, poised to escape, then settled back. Maybe she could help. Hobby probably was one of the people working in the house and maybe Mrs. Dees wasn't. If Mrs. Dees wasn't there, Hobby would let her help. As she wondered, a saw blade whizzed by her ear. Never had she moved so fast! She scrambled and stared. Back and forth, back and forth came the saw. A strange sort of now-you-see-it-now-you-don't magic show. The sawing stopped and began again at a different angle. Slowly she realized they were sawing a chunk out of the floor and that any min-ute a hole would open above her.

Crab-walking, she moved out of the way to watch. When they lifted the chunk of floor, she ducked behind the next pillar. Peering from be-hind the pillar, she saw three sets of legs, two sets in jeans and one in turquoise pants.

"What's that?" Mrs. Dees's voice. Those were her turquoise legs. She wore wonderful bright colors.

Nealy was so accustomed to owning this underpart of the house that she felt invaded. There were three faces staring down through the hole at her box: Mrs. Dees, Hobby, and another man. There was no escape route. They hadn't seen her yet, but she was trapped.

"Would you hand that up, please?" Mrs. Dees said.

Feet first, then legs, then a whole, Hobby descended through the hole. Nealy saw him see her, but he gave no sign as he lifted her box and passed it up through the hole and climbed after.

Above, he made distracting banter, and Nealy knew he was giving her the chance to "get the soot out." She got.

Now Nealy had more trouble than just the cleaning of more soot off her things. How had her life turned on her so fast? Taking Mama's jewelry box, getting herself accused of setting Mrs. Dees's house on fire, and having her stuff found under Mrs. Dees's house. It would be better if Godzilla got her. If he threw her into the sea, this would all be over. If he let her go or she escaped or was rescued, everyone would be so relieved they would forgive her anything.

Wouldn't they?

Once more she scrubbed herself, not forgetting her eyelids and inside her ears. Then she scrubbed the tub and put the clothes in the washer. Soot! She was going to wear out the washing machine with soot.

When she was finally done and dressed she left, batting the crystal into a wild whirling.

As quickly as she could, and without barking, meowing, chirping, or even seeing, she walked away from her house. At least there was the tree. If not the glory of the real tree, there was at least the one she had created in the street. True, she couldn't see it standing tall and reaching out to embrace the sky as she approached, but it helped to know it was there. A symbol of something.

Coming closer, she strained to see it ahead.

It wasn't there.

It had been painted over, asphalt black.

Walking past, to the corner of King Street, she was as close as she ever came to crying. She didn't even have the heart to stomp and say "soot, soot, soot." And it wasn't Godzilla who almost got her, but some fool boy whizzing by on a bicycle.

"Watch where you're going, jerk!" she shouted after him, ready to grab him and stomp him and blame him for everything. Everything. The jewelry box, the fire, Noel Anne, Grandma's being dead, Daddy's leaving, the deaths of the uncles who had died before she and Noel Anne were even born, *and* the tree. Both trees. The real one and the painted one.

Only when the boy was three blocks down the street did she see the bike. Blue. Bright light blue. Mrs. Dees's bicycle. Nealy was sure of it.

11
Thousands of Nails

Instantly, she was running, but just as she got going the boy on the bike turned a corner. By the time she reached that corner, there was no boy, no bike, nothing moving on the street. He could be anywhere by now.

Staring down the street, she watched for any movement, listened for any sound, a door opening or closing. Could she tell Mrs. Dees or the police that she'd seen the bike zooming past on King Street? When she remembered the geography of the area, Nealy brightened. Hanover became a peninsula on this south end, bounded by two rivers, and the only way out was across the marsh to the highway and the river bridge. If the boy pedaled down this way, he probably lived nearby.

For Nealy these streets were, as Grandma would say, old familiars. But down here, each house backed up to an alley, and she had never walked down the alleys. They were used for garages and garbage collection and were public property, but seemed private. And except for under Mrs. Dees's house, Nealy respected private property. She ducked into the nearest alley. This was new territory for her, and new dogs barked from new backyards, new birds sang from new trees, and new cats walked the top support beams of new wooden fences. But there was no blue bicycle.

At the end of the block, she crossed over and animal-talked her way down the next alley. If she had to walk every street and every alley, she would find that bike. Unless, she thought, it had been concealed inside a house or garage.

At the third yard in the second alley, there was the blue bike, propped against the back of the house. She ducked, as though someone was looking at her the same way she was looking at the bicycle. Then she peered through the fence, wishing she could see if the back fender had the HAVE

YOU HUGGED YOUR BIKE TODAY? sticker. She was sure it was Mrs. Dees's bike. There were lots of blue bicycles, but she'd never seen another one precisely this shade of bright light blue.

Now what should she do? Tell the police, or tell Mrs. Dees, who might not believe her? She was reluctant to walk away, afraid the bicycle would disappear. She looked left and right, thinking she could send someone with a message, but there was no one. These summer days were empty. Parents were at work and children were at day camp or day care.

Warily, she moved along the fence until she was out of sight of the bicycle; then, she quickly peeked back. It was still there. No one was moving toward it. No one was moving anywhere. She was alone in all the world.

As fast as she could without getting a stitch in her side, she ran home and called the police.

She didn't ask for Daddy, but that was who came. Daddy and his partner, Brian.

"You?" she said. She had seen more of Daddy this week than in the last two months.

"If a call comes in about my family, they let me know at once."

"Really?" she said. So that's why he had been

the one who came when Mama called the police about Noel Anne. The information comforted her somehow, made her feel that he was looking out for them more than she'd thought he was. She told them about the bike.

"Come show us," Brian said, opening the back door of the patrol car for Nealy.

She hesitated. She wasn't drawn to police action, or even to fires, unless one was in her face.

"I told you where it is."

"We need for you to show us," Brian said. "We have no search warrant and we have no reason to be looking, except for a citizen's report."

"I'm a citizen?"

The men laughed. "Of course you are," said Daddy.

Yes. Of course. She knew she was.

Brian drove south and swung the patrol car into the alley. For some reason, Nealy felt like a criminal again. Why did she feel like she was doing something wrong? What if the bike was gone? What if it wasn't Mrs. Dees's bike? What if she accused someone who hadn't done anything wrong, just as Mrs. Dees had accused her?

But there it was, and the three of them looked out from the police car at the bike.

"It's blue, all right. You stay here." Daddy and Brian stepped casually out of the car.

"It has a sticker on the back fender that says HAVE YOU HUGGED YOUR BIKE TODAY?" she said.

"What?" Daddy laughed. "Really?"

"Really." If Hobby had been here, he might have said, "Really, Nealy?"

As the men opened the gate and walked through the yard, Nealy watched as though they were heading for a gunfight. And, of course, they might be. Things could turn dangerous quickly for police officers. The two walked to the back of the house and looked at the bike. Then Brian walked around front while Daddy knocked on the back door. Nealy sucked in her breath when a woman came to the back door. Then a man appeared behind her. Then the boy. Daddy stayed there and Brian came back to the car.

"Let's go get Mrs. Dees," he said. "We have to have her identification."

"Didn't it have the sticker?"

"Oh, yeah," he said, heading for Dartmouth Street. "There's no doubt it's her bike. But when we don't have a warrant, we have to have positive ID from the owner. Getting Mrs. Dees will be faster than getting a warrant."

Mrs. Dees's car was still at the house. Hobby and the other man were gone. Brian took the stairs two at a time and Nealy scampered to keep up. He gave a hard rap on the door and his fist went through. Nealy jumped and Brian looked absolutely astonished as he examined his hand. The door was as thin as Hobby had said it was.

Brian stepped to a window and hollered. There were some voracious sounds from inside that Nealy recognized as the tearing-out of walls.

"She won't ever hear you above that racket," Nealy said, stepping over the windowsill. Enough of the walls had been ripped out so that they could see through the skeleton of part of the house, but they did not see Mrs. Dees. Nealy moved toward the noise. Brian followed.

In a small room with pipes sticking out of the floor, obviously a bathroom, Mrs. Dees was attacking the wall with a crowbar. She looked up at Nealy with irritation and puzzlement, then saw Brian and lowered her arm and dangled the crowbar from her hand.

"Your bike," Brian said. "Nealy's found it."

"You have? She has? Really? Where?" Mrs. Dees's face brightened as Brian told her.

"We need you to come identify it."

Mrs. Dees set the crowbar across the seat of the blackened commode and walked toward the door. Holding her arms out, she looked at herself. "I can't get into your car like this."

"Of course you can," Brian said. "We've had a lot worse in there, believe me."

As soon as they pulled up in the alley behind the house, Brian asked, "What do you think?"

Daddy was still standing there, safe, but surrounded by the family. The man, the woman, the boy and, now, several other children. All staring.

"Looks like it," Mrs. Dees said.

"Come identify it." Brian stepped out of the car and opened the back door for Mrs. Dees.

"Bring it here," Mrs. Dees said, standing by the car.

"We can't touch it until you have identified it," he said.

"You mean you want me to go in there?"

Nealy was glad she didn't have to go. Just watching from here made her nervous enough.

"I know it's hard, but otherwise we'll have to go back for a search warrant."

Brian opened the back gate, and as Mrs. Dees

started through she looked back at Nealy and held out a hand. Nealy leaped from the car and grabbed it.

The people by the house didn't say a word. They just stood, looking so accusing.

Nealy couldn't look at them. She wanted to run. She wondered if Mrs. Dees felt the same. They kept hold of each other's hands.

When they were close enough, Mrs. Dees said quietly, "This is it."

"You sure?" asked Brian.

"I'm sure," Mrs. Dees said.

"I'm sure, too," Nealy said.

Mrs. Dees looked at her.

"I know you had that sticker on the fender," she said.

Mrs. Dees also pointed out the bike chain with the blue plastic casing and a bracket on the handlebar that had once held a rearview mirror.

"We're taking this bike," Brian said. The parents didn't protest. Did they know that maybe their son had stolen this bike? Maybe burned a house?

Daddy rolled the bike along as they recrossed the yard.

"I'll ride it," Nealy offered as they neared the gate.

"We've got it," Brian said.

With moves so smooth Nealy was surprised, Daddy got in the passenger seat, shut the door, rolled down the window, and reached out to grip the bike when Brian lifted it. Even though it was certainly Mrs. Dees's bike, Nealy was still stupidly unsure and Mrs. Dees looked dismayed, too.

"Don't worry about it," Daddy said. "The kid probably did it. That family is a mess. We think the father sells anything the kids steal. He's like Fagin in *Oliver Twist*. When the call came in, every officer on duty wanted to answer it."

"Really?"

As Brian drove back to Mrs. Dees's house, Daddy held the bike as if it were easy.

"Well, you have your bike back," Brian said, smiling, as he sat it on the sidewalk for Mrs. Dees. "I'm sorry we can't give you back your house."

"Thanks, Mary Neal," Daddy said. Pleasure warmed her.

"Yes, thank you, Mary Neal," Brian said.

"Yes, Nealy. Thank you," said Mrs. Dees as she rolled the bike toward the porch and lifted it up the five steps. Daddy and Brian drove away.

"Are you going to make your house back?" Rebuilding the house seemed impossible, but how happy Nealy would be if it could be done.

"I'm going to try," Mrs. Dees said. "It's probably a bad idea, but I love this house. It has a spirit of its own."

"I know," Nealy said. "I don't think it's a bad idea at all." She wanted to say "I love this house, too," but she didn't dare.

Mrs. Dees opened the door, glancing, puzzled, at the hole in it.

"Brian—the police officer—put his fist through it."

"You could put your finger through it, I think." She rolled her bike into the house and Nealy followed. "Look," she said, showing Nealy the inside of the door. From the outside it had looked okay, but inside it was so deeply charred that Mrs. Dees raised a leg and smashed her foot through it. Except for the heavier outside frame, the door crumbled.

"Well, I'd better close it to keep things out." She closed the door frame and it even clicked shut. "Anything could get in here. Wild horses could come right in." She turned and walked between the studs down the hall to the bathroom. Mesmerized and smiling to herself, Nealy followed.

Mrs. Dees picked up the crowbar and resumed smashing and pulling down chunks of burned wall.

"It *is* like a death," she said, stopping for a moment. Her voice was distant and dreamy, as though she was talking to the inside of herself. As though Nealy weren't right there, listening. With a fierce blow, she embedded the crowbar in the wall and let it hang there as she sank to the toilet seat.

"I've lost my house," she said. "I've lost my nest." Then she sat, silent.

Nealy thought she should leave, but she didn't want to make a sound, not even a footstep. The least movement, she thought, would be disruptive, like waking someone from a too-sound sleep. She simply waited, surrounded by the blackened debris, until Mrs. Dees's silence and stillness began to frighten her.

"Mrs. Dees?"

The woman jumped as if wakened. "What? Nealy?"

"Mrs. Dees, are you all right?"

"Oh, did I go catatonic on you?"

"You got all still and quiet," Nealy said. "Is that catatonic?"

"Yes, actually, it is. I just go into a stupor. I've been doing that since the fire. It's the shock. I'll be here pulling nails and just stop in mid-pull." Mrs. Dees picked up a hammer, stood, and demonstrated catatonia, with the hammer ready to pull a nail but not pulling. "Hobby and C.J. realize I've stopped and call to me and tell me what I was supposed to be doing. I'll get over it."

Ah, Nealy thought. The other pair of legs she had seen belonged to someone named C.J. Eyes roving, she examined the area. Hundreds of narrow, horizontal strips of rough wood the size of lattice strips covered the walls and the ceiling, and broken ones littered the floor. Where they'd been burned or ripped away, there was a continuous row of small nails, about an inch apart, in the stud.

"What are all those nails?"

"Every one of them has to be pulled," Mrs. Dees said.

"Why?" Nealy asked. Thousands of nails paraded up every stud and across every ceiling joist. "How could you ever pull them all?"

"One at a time."

"Wouldn't it be easier to hammer them in?"

"We can't put up new wallboard until these

walls are all ripped out and the nails removed."
With three whacks, Mrs. Dees hammered one nail
in and with one pull, she took it out. The pull
was faster. "Also, if I nailed them in, they would
interfere with the new nails for the Sheetrock."

"What were they for?"

"Lathing strips. The wall was plaster, and those
wooden strips were nailed to hold the plaster."

"Whew," Nealy said. These wood strips rep-
resented thousands and thousands of nails. End-
less. Impossible. She looked at Mrs. Dees,
wondering if things were okay between them
now. Had Mrs. Dees given up the idea that she
was the one who had torched the house? Would
she let her hang around?

"It is like a death," Mrs. Dees said. "I didn't
think it was, because there was no loss of life. No
one was hurt. Even the cat was safe." She looked
at Nealy and shrugged. "I have always been a
bounce-back sort of person, but I have lost my
bounce."

Nealy didn't know what to say, but in a minute,
she said, "I'll help."

12
Best Day

The instant Mama was out the door to go to work on Thursday, Nealy, hammer in hand, was out the door to Mrs. Dees's. Hobby's orange truck was in Mrs. Dees's driveway. She ducked under the tape, then over a windowsill. Hobby and another man were tacking plywood down over the hole they'd cut in the hall floor.

"Have you met C.J.? C.J., Nealy. Nealy, C.J." The two men walked back into the living room and began to saw out a charred section of the living room floor. Then, with a hole cut to give a starting place, the men took to the floor with crowbars.

"Most of the floor can be saved," Hobby said between savage wrenching sounds. "But this end and all the hall will have to be replaced. That sucker poured kerosene from the front door to the back and dropped a match."

Nealy thought of the "sucker."

"Did you know we found Mrs. Dees's bicycle?" she asked.

"Yes, we saw it when we came in." Nealy looked around. There it was, near the patch of plywood where the footprints had been.

"Oh, is that what you cut out yesterday? The footprints?"

"Yeah, well, the state fire examiner cut out another piece of the floor after I cut out the footprints. They're so marvelously spooky. Besides, we have to cut out all the charred places before we spray."

"Spray?"

"Yeah, to get rid of the smoke smell. There's this special solution you can spray to absorb the smoke smell; otherwise, it would be here forever. You'll see us dressed like astronauts when we do it, because it's highly toxic and it drifts everywhere. Anyway, where did they find Mrs. Dees's bike?"

"I found it." She felt like a hero, telling them the story. Then, embarrassed, she moved to the studs to start pulling nails. The nails were so close together that it was hard to get the claw of the hammer around one. As she struggled Hobby came over and took the hammer from her.

"Here, let me show you. Start at the bottom and get the first nail out of the way; then, work up from below each nail." With a rocking motion on the curved claw end of the hammer, he see-sawed up to each subsequent nail and cleared the stud with amazing ease. "Here, I'll take the bottom nails out for you." Almost as quickly, he pulled the lowest nail from the studs all the way across one side of the room. "That ought to get you started."

It did. While Hobby and C.J. ripped out the damaged floor and covered it with plywood so no one would fall through, she pulled nails up each stud to as high as she could reach.

When Mrs. Dees drove into the driveway, Nealy stopped with hammer poised. Having been catatonic yesterday, maybe Mrs. Dees didn't remember their warm feelings. At least, Nealy had felt warmed. But now, standing frozen, she knew what being catatonic felt like.

"Okay, Nealy, you're pulling nails, remember?"

Hobby said to her. By the time Mrs. Dees stepped onto the porch, she was in motion again.

"Well, Nealy, what are you doing here?" Mrs. Dees said.

"We've got us an extra worker," Hobby said.

"I'm pulling nails," Nealy said, gesturing to the area she'd already worked.

"Ah," said Mrs. Dees. "We'll make a great team. That stooping part is hard for me." Immediately, she picked up a hammer and started where Nealy had left off, dragging an aluminum ladder over to reach above her as she yanked nails up to the top of the stud and started across the ceiling.

"Mrs. Dees, we'll get those from the ceiling," Hobby said.

"No, no," she said. "You're here to do all those things I can't do. Which is most of it. This I can do."

"It will take forever," he said.

"Yes, so it seems." They all stopped to look at the multitude of nails.

"I figure there are over six thousand nails per room," Hobby said. "Less for the bathrooms and more for the living room."

"One at a time," Nealy said.

"How does a dollar an hour sound to you, Nealy? What time did you start?"

"Oh, no, ma'am. I just came to help. I don't want to get paid." She was progressing up another row of nails.

"But I insist," Mrs. Dees said. "Volunteer time is over. Except for me, it's paid work from now on. Besides, I know you'll want more field guides."

Nealy sucked in her breath at the reminder that Mrs. Dees had her box of stuff. And, obviously, she knew whose it was. Nealy thought of the field guides, the insect collection, the jewelry box. Thinking of the jewelry box made her shudder. Diligently, she kept pulling nails, trying without success to pull her feelings loose. Somehow she had to square that with Mama.

Between Mrs. Dees up high, Nealy in the middle, and Hobby and C.J. below on the floor, the work crisscrossed until the men moved out onto the porch and began ripping out the charred porch ceiling. Nealy paused and rubbed her hand. What was that saying of Grandma's? "The spirit is willing but the flesh is weak." She had never understood it before but now she did. Her spirit was willing to keep pulling nails, but her arm and hand were not.

Mrs. Dees put her hammer down. "Come with me, Nealy. There's something I want to show you."

"Where are we going?"

"Just come on along. You'll be interested." Mrs. Dees started off down Dartmouth Street. Automatically, Nealy barked at the McHues' boxer and imitated the clear whistle of a cardinal. Realizing it was unusual behavior, she glanced at Mrs. Dees.

"You're quite an interesting person, Nealy."

Nealy stretched her legs and tried to match Mrs. Dees stride for stride.

"I knew you'd been coming under my house," Mrs. Dees said. "I just didn't know you had a collection under there."

Nealy lost her pace and also lost her practiced poker face. Adrenalin surged and she wanted to run.

"Such a fine collection, too."

Mrs. Dees was smiling. This was the first time since the fire that she'd seen Mrs. Dees smile. They approached the spot where the tree had been, where the painted tree had been. Before Nealy could be sad, she saw it.

The tree had been repainted in the street.

"Who did that?" But she knew the answer, the only answer. The tree was the same color she had painted it: Everglade. Hobby had painted it.

Mrs. Dees winked. "Hobby and I repainted it. But we don't want to be caught admiring it too much, do we, in case anyone from the city is watching. Thanks for the idea. I'm glad I could get in on it. I needed something like this." At that, Mrs. Dees turned and started back. She whistled at a Carolina wren.

"I apologize for being so rude to you the other day, Nealy, but I was so upset."

"Yes, ma'am, I know."

"I still am. I don't know who burned my house and it made me feel hateful toward anyone who might have."

"Yes, ma'am. I know."

"That doesn't mean it's fair," she said. "It isn't fair. It's just the way it is."

"Yes, ma'am," Nealy said again.

"Nealy, I like your interest in the field guides. And those drawings! You have a special talent."

For a moment, she wondered how Mrs. Dees knew about her drawings. But then she realized her small sketchbook was still in the box. She bit her lip. She knew she had a special talent, but when Mrs. Dees said it, she couldn't even get another "yes, ma'am" out.

"I hope you will always do the best for yourself, Nealy. Life tries to get in the way sometimes, but it's important for you to be your own best self."

At the house, the porch was littered with burned lumber torn from the ceiling, and Hobby and C.J. were once again covered with soot. They kicked a path through the debris for Mrs. Dees and Nealy.

"Oh, soot!" Nealy said, stamping and giggling.

"Oh, soot yourself," Hobby said, pretending he was going to rub his hands on her hair.

"We're cutting for lunch," Hobby said.

Just then Mama drove by, coming home for lunch.

"Me, too, I guess," Nealy said, glancing after Mama's car, stricken about the jewelry box, and about Mama calling her "best girl."

Mrs. Dees, who'd gone in, stepped back through the doorway with Nealy's box. "You'll want to take this along with you. This is not a good place for it right now. I've added to your collection. Something I think you'll like."

The shirt was folded on top of everything else,

and as Nealy walked down the steps she lifted the shirt to look under it. Just beneath it was a book, *Animals of the San Diego Zoo.* Nealy turned quickly, saying, "Tha-a-nks," but Mrs. Dees was not there. She wanted to go back and say thanks, but the knowledge of what she had to do with Mama pulled her forward.

"What do you have now?" Mama attacked the instant Nealy walked in. "Take that right back out. You know you can't bring animals into this house."

"No, no. It's just some of my stuff," Nealy said. "But I need to talk to you about something." She was going to take the box to her room, but Mama stopped her.

"What stuff? Just set that down right there."

Nealy set down the shirt-wrapped package. Instead of waiting for Mama to come look and make it happen, she lifted out the jewelry box.

"Where did you get that?" Mama was delighted, obviously thinking that Nealy had found it somewhere, rescued it, and brought it home.

Nealy took a huge breath. "I'm the one who took it, not Noel Anne."

Mama's face changed from pleasure to puzzlement to understanding. Her voice shrieked off the high end of the decibel scale. "And you let me think Noel Anne took it?"

"I tried to tell you." Nealy was ready to defend herself and say more, but her excuse sounded so feeble that no more words came out.

"Nealy, I just can't believe this. What's got into you? You're getting more like your sister every day. What am I going to do with you?"

"I don't know," Nealy mumbled. Her chin was on her chest. She saw the length of herself, down the buttons of her shirt to her dirty white sneakers. There was no way to avoid Mama's barrage. She didn't really want to avoid it, she just wanted to get it over with.

"Nealy, answer me." Mama grabbed her chin and forced it up, but Nealy kept her eyes down. "Look at me, young lady. You look at me when I'm talking to you. How could you do such a thing? How could you do this to me?"

"I didn't do it to you, Mama."

"That's got to be one of the dumbest answers I've ever heard. Who do you think you did it to, then?"

"To myself."

"To yourself. What kind of answer is that? It is *my* jewelry box. One of the few things I have of Mama's. Why did you do this?"

Nealy remembered how quickly and totally Mama had disposed of Grandma's things, not even asking Nealy or Noel Anne if they wanted anything of their grandmother's. Just getting rid of things, as though that would get rid of the pain.

She stared at the cranes under Mama's hands—the elegance of the long necks, long feathers, and long legs, the red blaze on the forehead.

Nealy shrugged. "I wanted it."

Now Mama examined the cranes, rubbing her fingers back and forth across the lacquered surface. Was she remembering Grandma and the day they had gone to Okefenokee and seen the cranes?

"But I would have given it to you."

They were surprising each other with their words. Bouncing the words between them. Slow lobs. Nealy gathered up breath and nerve and courage.

"No, you wouldn't have." The real birds were up to four feet tall and had a wingspan of over seven feet. Grandma, who never disturbed animals, had shouted at the cranes to stir them into

134

flying so Nealy could see that wingspan. "I'm sorry I took it. I shouldn't have taken it. It was wrong for me to take it. But you didn't let us keep anything of Grandma's. This is the only thing you kept."

Mama puffed a few sighs. Almost snorts. Standing, she stared at Nealy for long, long seconds. She sucked her lips between her teeth and made them thin and tight. As Nealy waited Mama turned and sank into a chair.

"You're right," she said. "I wouldn't have."

Nealy watched the crystal, which was turning slowly, in search of rainbows.

"Mary Neal, I've lost too much. I just didn't want reminders." One tear slipped out and slid down Mama's left cheek. Mama never cried.

"Noel and Neal," Mama said, naming her twin brothers, who had both been killed in Vietnam.

"Your father." Nealy steeled herself for the torrent that usually followed any mention of Daddy.

"Mama."

Nealy's eye fastened on the Tallahassee cityscape and started wandering the streets, but she called herself back. This was a time to pay attention.

"Noel Anne." Mama surprised Nealy with this addition to the list of losses.

Nealy backed away until she was leaning against the wall. "Mama, you didn't have to lose Noel Anne."

She wondered if she could draw silence.

Finally Mama gave another sigh-snort. "Mary Neal, I give you the lacquered box. But there has to be some compensation for stealing. Do you have any suggestions?"

"Anything, Mama. I'll do anything. I shouldn't have taken it and I shouldn't have let you think Noel Anne took it and I'll do anything to make it up to you." She rushed her words, more nervous now than when she'd taken it, wanting to do anything to have peace with Mama.

"Anything?" Mama asked.

Hurry up and get it over with, Nealy thought. What punishment could Mama possibly give? Nealy already did everything she could around the house. And she knew Mama wouldn't ground her, because Mama said that grounding turned out to be more punishment for herself. As long as she knew her daughters weren't getting into trouble, or going out when she said they couldn't, Mama liked having them out of the house.

"Mary Neal, what I want you to do," Mama said, "is ask Noel Anne to come home."

"Mama, really? You mean it?" Colors shimmered inside her, all red and blue and yellow and green. Then a purple shadow moved among the other colors.

"No, Mama. You have to do that." She pressed her lips together, wanting, too late, to contain her words. Mama wouldn't.

An enormous rumble made her jerk her head around before she opened her mouth again. "The tree cutter!" she shouted as she saw the heavy machinery that thundered past. "I've got to go," she said, and she was out the door.

As she ran she shouted, "Hobby! Mrs. Dees!" to the open windows. She saw Hobby come out a window as she streaked down the block. As fast as she ran, the men were already setting up the PEOPLE-AT-WORK signs and stringing the yellow tape lettered DANGER PEOPLE AT WORK DO NOT CROSS.

"You stay out of the way, missy," one man said. "We're going to be taking down this tree."

"Nooo!" Nealy screamed, and she ducked under the tape and scrambled into the tree before he could grab her.

"Oh, come on down. Don't give us any grief," the man said, and when she didn't, he reached out toward her. As he reached for her Hobby leaped into the tree behind her and gave her a boost. With her sneakers flat against the tree for traction, she scrambled up farther and draped herself over a branch like huge fruit.

Hobby returned to the ground, talking with the man. A worker climbed into the bucket and raised himself up to eye level with her.

"Climb on down, sweetheart. You don't want to get hurt." When she didn't, he turned on the saw.

Surely he wouldn't really start cutting the tree with her in it, would he? He was only trying to scare her. Just the same, the deafening buzz nearly shook her off her perch. Pressing herself into the tree for balance, she lowered her head so she could put her fingers in her ears. A commotion below caught her eye. There was Mrs. Dees, trying to reach the tree, but one of the men was holding her arm. Mrs. Dees angrily shook the man off and climbed up that first, easy, sloping part of the tree. Both the man and Mrs. Dees looked fierce. As she settled herself into the lowest fork of the tree, Mrs. Dees looked up and gave Nealy a thumbs-up.

Then came the other kids, swarming the tree, climbing up past Mrs. Dees. Lisa forged up toward Nealy while Mike, Josh, and Bobby climbed and crawled way up and out onto the overhanging limbs. The noise of the saw muffled Nealy's cheering. When she looked down, there were several people looking up. The Lyles. The McHues. Ms. Royster. And here came Mama, up to the back of the growing crowd.

And now, here came the police. And not only the police, but—wouldn't you know?—Daddy and Brian. Someone must have called Daddy in particular and said something that began with, "Your daughter . . ." The workman in the bucket turned off his saw and lowered himself to the ground. And—wouldn't you know?—who climbed into the bucket with the man but Daddy, and up they came. Could they get close enough to her for Daddy to pull her out of the tree?

"Come on now, Mary Neal. Be reasonable," he said, trying to talk her down. Close in front of his chest, so the other man in the bucket could not see, he was giving her a thumbs-up and then the okay circle. "You know you can't stay up here forever, so why don't you just come on down now?"

To go along with his words, she shouted, "Nooo! I'm not coming down, no matter what you say. I'm not going to let them take down this tree, even if I have to live here." A cheer roared out from the human fruit of the tree.

Someone began to chant, "Save our tree! Save our tree!" and the people in the tree and those below took it up.

"Save our tree! Save our tree!"

Daddy looked at the other man and shrugged, and the bucket was lowered. At the bottom, they conferred with the other workers and Brian.

The tree people didn't stop shouting, "Save our tree!" They would save this tree; Nealy was certain of it. Then the next and the next and the next. Let the city plant ten thousand trees, but let them leave these huge old oaks alone. Let them put more curves into the streets instead of taking them out.

She and Lisa exchanged a friendly glance, and Nealy looked down at Mrs. Dees and Mama. It might not always be this way with Mama, but for now it was good.

A ring of neighbors now surrounded the tree, some of them joining in the shout, "Save our tree! Save our tree!" And there was Daddy, pretending that he was trying to figure out what to do. The only one missing was Noel Anne, and surely, surely, Mama would have her home soon.

About This Book

In 1984, when my house was gutted by an arson fire, someone immediately said, "I'll watch for the book." Having experienced the trauma once, however, I didn't intend to relive it through writing. Judith Viorst says that recovering from grief takes longer than you ever think it will. It did. For reasons I still don't fully understand, this was the most horrendous thing that has ever happened to me.

The characters in my novel are alive to me, so I think what they think, laugh when they laugh, and hurt when they hurt. Everyone who knew me knew I had hurt enough over that fire. I was not going to write about it.

But, blessedly, time passes and I thought maybe I could finally write about it without it becoming *my* fire. The challenge of saying something about my adult experience with fire in a novel for children was solved by creative magic. An imaginary girl named Nealy crawled under my house and began to help me with a story.

I gave Mrs. Dees ceramics and clay sculpture instead of writing. I made up characters, combined real ones and, of necessity, left out some. I didn't think anyone would be interested in a twenty-volume set, least of all my editor!

Intending to be supportive and kind, several people suggested that the fire was a blessing in disguise. No! It was not. Though generosity rained on my head, I did not, do not, and will never think of the fire as a blessing.

After the fire, many splendid serendipities happened, which led a friend to say, "I can't believe the miracles you're having in the face of disaster." *Yes!* This is true.

In the rush of help during those first days, my daughter said to me, "Mom, if we ever in our entire lives feel alone and friendless, all we need to do is remember this."

D.B.S.